CHARACTER-DRIVEN DRAMA

"Some bonds are meant to break, so we can grow into who we are meant to be."

Roshawn Nixon

Copyright © 2025 by Roshawn Nixon. All rights reserved. No portion of this publication may be reproduced or transmitted in any form or by any means without the prior written permission of the copyright own

DEDICATION

To those who walk alongside us in life, through the joys and the struggles, the quiet moments and the loud ones. To friends, old and new, who remind us that even as we change, we are never alone.

This book is for the ones who helped shape me into who I am today, and for those I have yet to meet—may our stories continue to unfold.

And to the past, for teaching me how to let go, and to the future, for showing me the way forward.

TABLE OF CONTENTS

PROLOGUE: THE FRACTURED THREADS — 1

THE GATHERING — 6

- CHAPTER I: THE INVITATION — 6
- CHAPTER II: THE FIRST MEETING — 22
- CHAPTER III: SHARED MEMORIES — 36
- CHAPTER IV: UNFINISHED BUSINESS — 49
- CHAPTER V: THE DIVISIONS — 61
- CHAPTER VI: A MOMENT OF CLARITY — 74

THE CONFRONTATION — 86

- CHAPTER VII: BITTER REVELATIONS — 86
- CHAPTER VIII: THE TURNING POINT — 94
- CHAPTER IX: THE BREAKING POINT — 107
- CHAPTER X: INTROSPECTION — 119
- CHAPTER XI: FULL CIRCLE — 131

SUMMARY — 138

ABOU T THE AUTHOR — 143

Prologue: The Fractured Threads

The night was unusually still for a summer evening in the quiet town. The air was thick with the heat of the day, but there was an undeniable chill that seemed to hover just beneath the surface. Sarah stood at the edge of the cabin's porch, staring out into the woods, the thick trees standing like silent sentinels in the fading light. Her mind was a mess of tangled thoughts, memories flashing like old photographs, and the weight of the years she had spent trying to hold onto something that was slipping through her fingers.

It had been almost ten years since they'd all been together—Jason, Emma, Tom, Ben, and her. Ten years since they had laughed without a care, since they had shared secrets and dreams that seemed unbreakable. She had been the glue, the one who held them together through all the changes, all the inevitable rifts that time created. But even she couldn't stop what was coming. Even she couldn't keep the group together when everything started to fall apart.

Tonight was supposed to be a reunion, a chance to reclaim what they had lost. But as Sarah stood there, feeling the weight of the world pressing down on her shoulders, she wondered if they could ever truly reclaim what had once been. The faces of her old friends, the faces that had once been so familiar, now seemed like strangers. Jason was still the same—charming, witty, always ready with a smile that masked the turmoil beneath—but there was something more hollow in his eyes now. Emma was quieter, softer, her laugh no longer the carefree sound that had once filled every room. Tom was different, too—more guarded, more defensive, a man who had been through too much and kept it all to himself. Ben had always been the one who drifted the furthest, the one who never fully let himself be a part of the group, and now, it seemed, he had finally let go.

She had brought them together because she believed that they could fix what had been broken. She had hoped that a few days together would be enough to repair the years of distance, to bridge the gaps that had formed between them. But now, with each passing hour, it was becoming clearer to Sarah that they were all too far gone. Too much had changed. Too much had been left unsaid.

The door behind her creaked open, and Sarah didn't need to turn around to know who it was. She could feel Emma's presence, like a quiet ripple in the air, pulling Sarah back into the present. Emma stepped up beside her, her eyes scanning the darkened woods, her posture stiff, as if she, too, was struggling to find a way back into the circle they had once shared.

"I didn't think it would be like this," Emma said softly, her voice barely above a whisper, as though she were afraid to speak too loudly in case the silence might crack. "I thought... I thought we could fix it."

Sarah didn't answer right away. She couldn't. She didn't know how to explain what she had been feeling since the moment they had all come together again. She had expected the old warmth to return, the closeness they once shared, but it had been replaced by a quiet tension, a wall that seemed impossible to tear down. They were all trying so hard to relive the past, to make the pieces fit, but the reality was that they had all changed—grown apart in ways they hadn't been prepared for.

"Maybe we can't," Sarah said finally, her words soft, but they hung heavy in the air. "Maybe we can't go back to what we were."

Emma looked at her, the sadness in her eyes unmistakable. "I don't know what I expected," she admitted. "Maybe a part of me thought that just being together again would be enough to make it all right. But it's not. It's like we're all pretending."

Pretending. The word lingered in the air, settling between them like a ghost. It was true. They were all pretending. Pretending that they could resurrect something that had long since died, pretending that the years they had spent apart hadn't changed them. Pretending that they were still the same group of friends, still bound by the same old loyalty, when, in truth, they had all grown into different people, with different needs, different pains, different dreams.

"I thought it would be enough too," Sarah admitted, her voice cracking slightly. "But maybe it's not. Maybe we're just... too far gone."

The words felt like a weight lifting from her chest, but at the same time, it was as if the ground beneath her was shifting, threatening to swallow her whole. The truth, as always, was painful. But it was also freeing. They couldn't go back. They couldn't fix everything that had been broken. And yet, in this painful realization, Sarah felt something stir within her—a small flicker of hope that perhaps there was a way forward, even if it wasn't the way she had imagined.

Emma's gaze softened, and she gave Sarah a small, sad smile. "We tried," she said quietly, as if offering Sarah some comfort. "We really tried."

The truth of it hit Sarah like a wave, and for a brief moment, she felt the weight of everything that had been lost—the years, the friendships, the parts of herself that she had given away, trying to hold onto something that was slipping through her fingers. But in that moment, as the night stretched out before them, something else began to settle in her heart. It wasn't relief, not exactly, but it was a kind of acceptance. She couldn't control what had happened. She couldn't fix it. But she could choose to move forward, to stop trying to turn back the clock, to stop chasing something that was gone.

"Maybe it's time to let go," Sarah whispered, more to herself than to Emma. The words felt foreign, but they also felt right.

Emma didn't answer, but Sarah could see the silent understanding in her eyes. They had both come to the same conclusion, even if they hadn't said it aloud before. The reunion wasn't about fixing the past. It was about finding a way to move forward, even if that meant accepting the pain, the loss, and the fact that some things couldn't be repaired.

The silence stretched between them, but it wasn't uncomfortable. It was a kind of peace, a moment of understanding that, no matter what had happened, they had done their best. They had tried to fix something that had been broken for too long. And now, it was time to let go and allow the future to unfold in its own way.

After a long moment, Emma spoke again, her voice gentle. "I think we need to stop pretending," she said softly. "We need to stop pretending that things can be the way they were. It's okay to let go."

It was a relief, hearing those words. The pressure that had been building in Sarah's chest seemed to ease just a little. Emma was right. They didn't need to pretend anymore. They could face the reality of what had happened and move forward, no matter how difficult that might be.

"I think I'm ready," Sarah said, her voice quiet but steady. "I'm ready to let go."

And with those words, the final piece of the puzzle clicked into place. She was ready. Ready to face the truth. Ready to face the future. Ready to stop chasing ghosts.

The group, the friends she had once known, would always be a part of her. They had shaped her in ways that she would carry with her forever. But it was time to accept that they were no longer the same people, and neither was she. The reunion, for all its hopes and expectations, had finally brought Sarah to the realization that it wasn't about fixing the past. It was about accepting the changes, embracing the new versions of themselves, and finding peace in what had been.

And with that peace, Sarah finally felt free.

The Gathering

Chapter I: The Invitation

The stillness of early morning settled over the protagonist's apartment. The faint hum of the city outside was muffled by the weight of silence within the room. Sarah stood in front of the window, staring out at the distant skyline. Her apartment was sparse—furnishings minimal, save for the necessities. As a single woman in her thirties, she had grown accustomed to solitude. Her days were filled with work at the marketing agency she ran, while the evenings were hers to do with as she pleased. Sometimes, she'd binge-watch old movies, sometimes read. But today, something felt different.

The quiet was shattered by the soft chime of her phone vibrating on the coffee table. A message. From an old friend.

Sarah picked up the phone, hesitating for a moment. The name that appeared on the screen made her heart skip a beat. It was Jason, one of the closest friends from her college days—someone she hadn't spoken to in over five years. The kind of friend who had once known her better than anyone else, yet the distance between them had grown as the years passed.

She tapped the message open. It was simple. A straightforward text that would have seemed trivial if it had come from anyone else.

"HEY SARAH, I'M ORGANIZING A REUNION THIS SUMMER FOR THE OLD GROUP. THOUGHT IT'D BE NICE TO CATCH UP. WOULD LOVE TO SEE YOU THERE. IT'S BEEN TOO LONG."

That was it. No pleasantries, no extended explanation. Just an invitation. A sharp reminder of the years that had slipped away unnoticed. Sarah stared at the screen, feeling an unexpected rush of emotions. Nostalgia for the past, curiosity about the present, and a small seed of anxiety about the possibility of confronting who she had become in the time since they'd all gone their separate ways.

She set the phone down, momentarily distracted by the memories that flooded in. The friends Jason referred to were not just casual acquaintances. They were family, the people who had shared her most formative years—her college experiences, her triumphs, and her failures. The friends who had celebrated her small victories and consoled her through the darkest of times. They were her group, the ones she had laughed with until her stomach hurt, the ones she had stayed up all night with, talking about everything and nothing. Back then, it had seemed like they would be inseparable.

But time had a way of changing things. Graduation, new jobs, new relationships, and new cities had slowly distanced them. What had once felt permanent had become fleeting. Sarah and Jason had drifted apart, then the others. Slowly, but inevitably, everyone had gone their own way.

Now, standing in her quiet apartment, Sarah felt torn. A part of her longed to return to those carefree times, to rekindle those friendships, to revisit the days when life felt simpler. But another part of her hesitated. Could she really step back into that world? Did she still fit in? Would she even recognize the people they had become?

Jason's text had opened a door to a past that was both comforting and unsettling. She imagined seeing them all again—how they had changed, how she had changed. Would they remember her the way she remembered them? Or had too much time passed, erasing the connection they had once shared?

After a few moments of contemplation, Sarah finally typed her response: "I'LL THINK ABOUT IT. THANKS FOR REACHING OUT."

Her thumb hovered over the send button for a moment before she pressed it. The message was neutral, non-committal. She wasn't ready to make a decision yet. But something about receiving the invitation stirred a yearning inside her—a longing to reconnect with the past, even if only for a brief moment.

She put the phone down, picked up her cup of coffee, and tried to focus on the tasks at hand. But the thought of the reunion lingered in the back of her mind.

As the day went on, Sarah couldn't shake the feeling of unease. She went about her usual routine, but the message kept coming back to her. Was she ready to face those old friends? More importantly, was she ready to face herself? The Sarah who had been part of that group was a version of herself she hadn't thought about in years. She had changed. Would they still recognize her? Or would she be just a stranger to them, someone who no longer belonged in their lives?

The anxiety of the unknown gnawed at her, but there was also a flicker of excitement. What if the reunion could be everything she had imagined and more? What if the old bonds could be rekindled, and she could feel like part of something again?

But then another thought occurred to her. What if the reunion exposed just how much they had all changed, how much they had outgrown each other? Maybe some things were better left in the past, where they belonged.

Later that evening, Sarah settled into her favorite armchair, a book in hand, but her mind was elsewhere. She could picture the group gathering, the familiar faces, the old dynamic between them all. She could hear their voices in her head, laughing, arguing, reminiscing about the good old days. It was all so vivid in her mind, yet so distant. Time had transformed those memories into something almost unreal.

The phone buzzed again, and she jolted out of her thoughts. This time, it was a group text, sent by Jason to all the old friends. He'd attached a group photo from their college days. The faces in the picture were so young, so carefree. It hit her harder than she expected—seeing those smiles, those familiar expressions. But now, looking at the photo, she realized just how much time had passed. How different everything was.

As Sarah stared at the group photo, memories began to flood her mind, carrying with them a mix of warmth and regret. The faces were the same, yet she could see the subtle changes that time had carved into them. Jason's infectious grin, Emma's playful wink, Tom's ever-present smirk—it was all there, but the context had changed. She wondered where they were now, what they had become.

She put the phone down, the weight of nostalgia pressing heavily on her chest. She hadn't realized how much she had missed them until this very moment. But what would it be like to see them again? The questions churned in her mind, pulling her in two directions: one wanting to hold onto the past, the other fearing what it might reveal.

A few minutes passed, and Sarah opened the group text again. The photo was accompanied by a brief message from Jason: "IT'D BE GREAT TO CATCH UP, NO PRESSURE IF YOU CAN'T MAKE IT. JUST TRYING TO GET THE GANG TOGETHER. LET'S SEE WHAT HAPPENS!"

His casual tone made it clear that he wasn't expecting anything more than a casual get-together. But to Sarah, it felt like so much more. The gang. That term had once been a symbol of endless possibilities, of friendships that seemed like they could withstand anything. But now, that phrase felt foreign. The bonds they once shared had been frayed by time and distance.

Still, she couldn't help but feel a pull. A tug of longing for the easy camaraderie they had once had. The reassurance that no matter where life took them, they would always have each other. But she knew that things were never that simple.

The next few days passed in a blur of indecision. Sarah went through the motions of her daily life, working, running errands, keeping up with her routine. Yet in the back of her mind, the reunion lingered like an unspoken question. Could she really go back to those people, those moments? Would it be a step forward, or would it drag her back to a time that was better left behind?

The weekend arrived, and she found herself sitting at her kitchen table, her laptop open, ready to make a decision. Her cursor hovered over the "reply" button in the group chat, and for a moment, she just stared at it.

What could she possibly say? What kind of answer would make sense?

"I'LL COME," she typed. She quickly deleted the message, then typed again. "I'M THINKING ABOUT IT." It wasn't a commitment, but it was progress.

Her finger hovered over the send button once more. A sigh escaped her lips as she thought of the many reasons not to attend. Maybe she wasn't ready to confront the people she used to be. Maybe their lives had moved on, and so had she. But deep down, there was a longing to reconnect, to see if the spark of their old friendships could still catch fire.

She hit send.

As soon as Sarah sent the message, she felt a sense of both relief and anxiety. It was out there now, the commitment, even if it wasn't fully made. Her mind began to race. What would the reunion be like? How would it feel to be in the same room with people who had once been her closest companions?

The next few days passed in a haze of anticipation. Jason responded to her message with a quick "AWESOME! WE'LL FIGURE OUT THE DETAILS SOON." His enthusiasm was palpable, and for a moment, Sarah felt a spark of excitement. But just as quickly, the doubts crept back in. Would she be able to reconnect with them? Would they still see her as part of the group?

Her phone buzzed again that evening, this time with a message from Emma.

"I HEARD YOU'RE COMING! THIS IS GOING TO BE AMAZING. I CAN'T WAIT TO SEE YOU AGAIN!"

Sarah smiled as she read Emma's message, but the feeling was fleeting. Emma had always been the optimistic one, the one who believed in the magic of friendships, no matter how much time had passed. But Sarah wasn't sure if it would be that simple.

She spent the rest of the night in a quiet fog, wondering how her friends had changed over the years. She thought of Jason, of Emma, of Tom—her mind wandered back to the days when they had been inseparable, when it felt like they could conquer anything together. But time had a way of doing things, didn't it? Time changed everything.

The following evening, as Sarah was cleaning up after dinner, her phone rang. It was an unfamiliar number, and she hesitated before answering.

"Hello?"

"Sarah?" It was Jason's voice, full of warmth and familiarity. "Hey, it's Jason. I just wanted to check in and see how you're feeling about the reunion. You still in?"

She hesitated, a slight tightness in her chest. "Yeah, I'm still thinking about it. I'll be there, I guess."

"Good. I'm really glad. Look, I know it's been a long time, but we all really want to see you again. I know things have changed, but I think we can make it work."

"I'm not sure what that means, Jason," Sarah said, her voice betraying a hint of anxiety. "What's going to happen at this thing? What are we supposed to do? Are we going to pretend like nothing's changed?"

Jason was quiet for a moment, and then he sighed. "I know, Sarah. I know it's weird. But we're just trying to reconnect. We're not expecting it to be like before, but we're hoping it's not as awkward as we might think. It's just... I don't know, it feels like we owe it to ourselves to try."

Sarah was silent, the words lingering in the air. Could it really be that simple? Could a group of old friends, each

with their own lives and their own struggles, simply pick up where they left off?

"I don't know, Jason," she said softly. "I'm just not sure."

"I get it," Jason replied. "Take your time. Just let me know if you change your mind."

With that, the call ended. Sarah stood still for a moment, staring at the phone in her hand. There was a deep longing in her chest, but also a profound uncertainty. Was this reunion going to be a bridge to the past or a stark reminder of how much had changed?

Sarah woke up the next morning with a knot in her stomach. The uncertainty from the previous night hadn't lifted, and it seemed to hang over her like a thick fog. She had agreed to attend the reunion, but the decision felt like both a relief and a heavy burden. What had she done? She couldn't help but wonder if she had made the right choice. Was it too late to change her mind?

But in her heart, she knew that backing out would mean losing the chance to reconnect with her past, with the friends who had once meant the world to her. She had to go, even if it felt uncomfortable. Even if it meant confronting parts of herself she wasn't ready to face.

The next few days felt like a waiting game. She found herself constantly checking her phone, half-expecting another message from one of the others. Jason had reached out to confirm the details of the reunion, which would take place over a weekend in a cabin just outside of town—an idyllic setting that seemed to promise a return to simpler times.

The weather forecast showed that it would be a warm, sunny weekend, perfect for the kind of laid-back gathering that they had enjoyed in their youth. There would be barbecues, late-night conversations, and the quiet rhythm of nature surrounding them. It sounded perfect, but the more Sarah thought about it, the more uncertain she became. Was she really ready for this? Could she fit back into their world after all this time?

That weekend, as Sarah packed her bags, she couldn't help but think of all the small details she had once obsessed over before attending any of their get-togethers. What should she wear? How should she act? What would everyone think? Those same anxieties had been present all those years ago, but back then, they had been paired with the carefree attitude of youth. Now, the stakes felt much higher.

Sarah packed light—a few casual outfits, some toiletries, and a journal. She didn't plan to write much, but she thought it would be nice to have it on hand, a way to reflect if the emotions became too overwhelming. She hesitated for a moment at the door, looking back at the apartment she had built for herself. Was this a temporary escape from her life, or would this weekend change everything?

It felt like she was about to step into another world, a world where the past and present would collide. She had changed. She had to accept that. But the question was whether her friends had changed as well. Were they still the people she had known so many years ago, or had they become strangers in the time that had passed?

The drive to the cabin was longer than Sarah had anticipated. As she navigated the winding roads, she couldn't help but notice the trees that seemed to blur by, a steady reminder of how time had changed everything around her. The landscape hadn't changed much, but everything still felt unfamiliar.

She pulled up to the cabin, and it didn't take long before she saw the familiar faces that she hadn't seen in years. Jason was the first to approach her, a warm smile spreading across his face as he saw her car.

"Sarah!" he exclaimed, walking toward her with open arms. "You made it!"

For a moment, Sarah felt the pressure melt away. Jason's presence was comforting, like a familiar anchor in the sea of uncertainty. She stepped out of the car and hugged him, feeling the weight of the past five years dissolve in that brief embrace.

"It's good to see you," she said, her voice slightly shaky.

"You too," Jason replied. "It's been way too long. Everyone's inside, getting things set up. Come on in, we're just getting started."

As they walked toward the cabin, Sarah's mind was racing. It had been so long since she had been in this kind of setting, surrounded by people who knew her so well. She didn't know what to expect, but she couldn't deny the excitement that bubbled up inside her. She was back in the fold, at least for this weekend.

The cabin itself was rustic, nestled on the edge of a small lake. Its wooden walls and stone fireplace gave it a cozy, nostalgic feel, one that seemed to embody the kind of retreat they had always dreamed of. The others were already there—Tom, Emma, and a few other familiar faces from their college days. The group was smaller than it had been in the past, but that somehow made it feel more intimate.

"Sarah!" Emma's voice rang out as she caught sight of her. She was standing by the grill, flipping burgers, her face lighting up when she saw her old friend. "I'm so glad you could make it!"

Sarah smiled, feeling a warmth spread through her at the sight of Emma. Emma hadn't changed much—her bright smile and infectious energy still the same as it had been in college. It felt like a small victory, being greeted by someone who still remembered her for who she used to be.

"Thanks for inviting me," Sarah said, walking toward her. "It's been too long."

"It really has," Emma replied. "We've missed you, Sarah."

Tom was standing by the picnic table, a beer in hand. His arms were crossed, and his usual smirk was in place. He looked the same, though there were subtle signs of aging—a few gray hairs at his temples, a hint of lines around his eyes. He glanced up as Sarah approached and gave her a nod.

"Hey," Tom said coolly, though his eyes softened when he saw her. "Didn't think you'd actually show up."

Sarah laughed, the sound easing some of her tension. "I didn't think I would either, honestly."

"I'm just glad you're here," he said, his tone lighter now.

The others chimed in with greetings, and Sarah felt a sense of ease begin to settle over her. They were all here, the gang from her past, the people who had once been her whole world. It was strange to see them again, but in some ways, it felt like no time had passed.

The first night of the reunion was easy. The group ate dinner together, shared stories, and laughed as though no time had passed. The conversation was effortless, moving from one topic to the next with a natural flow. Sarah could see how everyone had changed—there was a sophistication to their conversation, an air of adulthood that hadn't been there before. They were still the same people, but they had grown up, just as she had.

As the night wore on, the group moved outside, gathered around a fire pit. The warmth of the fire seemed to wash over them, pulling them closer together. The crackling of the flames filled the silence as the group settled in, each of them holding a drink in their hand, looking out at the stars.

Jason broke the silence. "It's crazy how we're all here again. I mean, after everything. It's like no time has passed, but at the same time, it feels like a lifetime ago."

Everyone nodded, the shared sentiment lingering in the air. It was true, there was an odd sense of both familiarity and distance. Sarah felt it too—like she was both part of the group and an outsider at the same time. But the warmth of the fire and the sound of laughter helped to ease the awkwardness. Maybe it wouldn't be so bad after all.

As the fire crackled and the conversation shifted from past memories to present updates, Sarah felt the weight of years melt away. The awkwardness of the initial reunion had dissipated, and the rhythm of old friendships seemed to return naturally. The group was now seated comfortably in a loose circle, the warmth of the fire flickering across their faces. Jason leaned back in his chair, hands resting behind his head, as he looked at everyone with a content smile.

"Remember when we used to stay up all night talking about the future?" Jason asked, his tone both nostalgic and amused. "I swear we had it all figured out back then."

Everyone chuckled, and for a moment, it felt like they were back in those late-night discussions, fueled by youthful optimism. The night air was crisp, and a gentle breeze whispered through the trees, adding to the sense of calm that had settled over the group.

"I don't think we ever had anything figured out," Sarah said, leaning back in her chair, a small smile tugging at her lips. "We just liked the idea of knowing everything."

"True," Emma added, her laughter contagious. "But I think we were just scared of the unknown. Now, look at us—most of us have jobs, mortgages, responsibilities. Who would've thought?"

"Yeah, adulthood hit us hard," Tom said with a grin. "I don't think I expected to be this responsible. But I guess it comes with the territory."

Sarah could feel the changes in the group, not just in the way they spoke, but in their mannerisms, their body language, the way they interacted. There was a confidence now that had been missing before. They were all adults, with their own lives and stories, and though the carefree nature of their past was still a part of them, it had been tempered by the experiences of life.

As the night wore on, Sarah found herself quietly observing the group. It was clear that time had shaped them, as it had shaped her. But despite the changes, there was an undeniable connection—a thread that still tied them together.

After a few hours of relaxed conversation, the group began to wind down. Some people retired to their rooms, while others lingered by the fire, continuing to chat in a more subdued tone. Sarah, however, felt a growing unease within herself. Despite the laughter and the warmth, there was a nagging feeling she couldn't shake—a feeling that perhaps the bond they once shared wasn't as strong as it had been.

She excused herself and wandered down to the lake, feeling the cool night air against her skin. The soft sound of the water lapping at the shore was soothing, and she took a deep breath, allowing herself to momentarily disconnect from the others.

As she stood there, her thoughts drifted back to the past, to the days when the group had been inseparable. She had been so sure of their place in her life, so confident that they would always be there. But now, standing by the lake, it felt like something had shifted, something that couldn't be undone. Perhaps they had outgrown each other, or maybe it was just her who had changed. It was hard to tell.

Her mind raced with thoughts of the future—the uncertainties of relationships, the fears of drifting apart. She had built a life for herself, one that didn't rely on the past. But here she was, questioning everything. Why had she come? Was it just out of a desire for comfort, for the familiar? Or was it because, deep down, she still craved the connection they had once shared?

As Sarah continued to gaze at the water, she heard footsteps approaching. She turned to see Emma walking toward her, a soft smile on her face. Emma had always been able to read Sarah better than anyone else, and Sarah suspected she knew exactly what was on her mind.

"Mind if I join you?" Emma asked, her voice gentle but knowing.

"Of course," Sarah replied, stepping aside to make room on the small dock. Emma sat down beside her, and for a moment, they both stared out at the dark water in silence.

"You've been quiet tonight," Emma said, her voice filled with understanding. "I can tell something's bothering you. Do you want to talk about it?"

Sarah hesitated. She had never been good at sharing her worries, especially when it came to her friends. But something about Emma's presence made it feel safer, easier.

"I don't know, Emma," Sarah said slowly. "It's just... everything feels different. I'm not sure I fit in here anymore. It's like we're all these different versions of ourselves now, and I don't know how to reconcile that with the past."

Emma nodded, her expression thoughtful. "I get it. It's been a while, and I think we've all changed in ways that we didn't expect. But that doesn't mean we can't still find something in each other, something worth holding onto."

"I know," Sarah said quietly. "But I guess I'm just scared that it won't be the same. That we won't be the same."

"We're not the same," Emma said with a soft laugh. "None of us are. But that doesn't mean we can't still have something meaningful. Maybe it won't be like it was before, but that doesn't mean it's any less important."

Sarah felt a wave of relief wash over her as Emma spoke. There was a wisdom in her words, a reassurance that she had been searching for without even knowing it. Perhaps the reunion wasn't about recapturing the past, but about creating something new. The idea of moving forward, of accepting the changes in their lives, was something Sarah hadn't fully considered.

"I guess I've been holding on to this idea of what we used to be," Sarah admitted, her voice soft. "I'm afraid that if we're not that anymore, there won't be anything left."

"There's always something left," Emma said, her voice steady. "The connections we have are deeper than what they seemed when we were younger. Maybe we just need to let them evolve with us."

Emma's words lingered in Sarah's mind as they sat together by the water. The night felt still, as though the world was holding its breath, waiting for Sarah to come to terms with what she had been avoiding. She knew that she couldn't go back to the past. But maybe, just maybe, she didn't need to.

The next morning, as the group gathered for breakfast, Sarah felt a shift inside herself. She wasn't sure what would happen next, but she was ready to give it a chance. The past was behind her, but the present was something she could still shape.

She found herself laughing more easily, engaging in conversations with the others without the weight of expectations hanging over her. The awkwardness that had marked her arrival was now gone, replaced by a tentative sense of belonging. Maybe this reunion wasn't about recapturing what had been lost; it was about finding new connections, new ways to be a part of each other's lives.

The day passed quickly, filled with light-hearted conversations, a few rounds of cards, and the kind of easy banter that had once come so naturally. There were moments of quiet reflection, but they didn't feel out of place. It was as if Sarah was learning how to navigate the space between the past and the present.

And as the sun began to set, casting a golden glow over the cabin and the lake, Sarah realized that maybe this reunion wasn't about finding the old friendships they had once shared. Maybe it was about discovering what those friendships could become.

Chapter II: The First Meeting

The morning of the reunion arrived with a gentle hum of anticipation in the air. Sarah had spent the night at the cabin, waking early to the sound of birds chirping and the faint rustle of leaves in the breeze. The previous evening had been filled with pleasant chatter and catching up, but now, as the sun began to climb higher in the sky, she couldn't help but feel the tension creep back into her chest. Today, the rest of the group would arrive. Today, the real reunion would begin.

Her hometown was just a short drive from the cabin, a small town nestled at the edge of a forested area, with winding roads that led to familiar places—places she hadn't visited in years. She could already feel the pull of nostalgia, the memories of her childhood and teenage years flooding her thoughts. The town hadn't changed much, but then again, neither had Sarah. At least, not on the surface.

The drive was quiet, a gentle solitude that gave Sarah time to reflect. She thought about the people she would see, the ones who had shaped so much of her younger years. The last time they had all been together was at their college graduation. After that, life had taken them in different directions—some staying close to home, others venturing far away. But now, here they were, coming back together in the same place where it had all started.

Sarah parked her car in the lot near the old café, the central meeting point for their reunion. It had been their usual hangout in high school and college, the place where they had spent countless afternoons sipping coffee, talking about their dreams, and making plans for the future. It seemed fitting that this would be the location to begin their reconnection.

She stepped out of the car, feeling a mixture of excitement and unease. The weather was perfect—clear skies, a light breeze, the kind of day that felt like it was waiting for something. She could see the café in the distance, its familiar brick façade standing proudly against the backdrop of the town. As she made her way toward it, Sarah felt her heart race. This was it. The first step into the past.

When Sarah entered the café, she was immediately hit by the familiar smell of freshly brewed coffee, mingling with the scent of pastries. The interior had barely changed—the same mismatched furniture, the quirky décor, the walls lined with old photographs of the town's history. It was comforting, but at the same time, it felt like stepping into a time capsule. The place was a snapshot of their youth, a reminder of who they had been.

She spotted Jason first, sitting at a corner table near the window. He was talking animatedly to Tom, who was lounging back in his chair with a mug of coffee in hand.

As Sarah approached, both men turned toward her, their faces lighting up with recognition.

"Sarah!" Jason called out, rising from his chair. His warm smile immediately put her at ease. "It's good to see you."

Tom gave her a small nod, his expression neutral but not unkind. "Hey, Sarah. Long time."

The awkwardness was palpable. There was a familiarity in the way they greeted her, but it wasn't the same as before. Something was different—unspoken, but clearly felt. The years between now and then had created a space that was hard to bridge, a gap that neither Sarah nor her friends knew quite how to cross.

Sarah smiled, trying to mask her own discomfort. "It's good to see you both," she replied, taking a seat across from them.

Jason cleared his throat, glancing toward the door. "The others should be here soon. I think Emma and the others are just getting settled in." He glanced back at Sarah with a hint of curiosity. "So, how's life been for you? I mean, after everything..."

Sarah hesitated for a moment, unsure of how to answer. So much had happened in her life—so much had changed—but she didn't want to delve too deeply into it just yet. Instead, she shrugged slightly, offering a vague smile.

"Life's been... fine. Busy. You know how it is."

Tom, sensing her reluctance to share too much, changed the subject. "Well, we've all been busy. But I think this reunion was a good idea. It's nice to be back here, in the old spot."

Sarah nodded, looking around the café. There was comfort in its familiarity, but also a strange sense of displacement. She couldn't help but wonder if she still belonged here, if she still fit in with the group.

The door to the café chimed, signaling the arrival of Emma and the others. Sarah turned to see her old friend walk in, her presence lighting up the room. Emma was just as she remembered—her curly hair bouncing with every step, her wide smile filling the room with warmth. Behind her were a few others—friends Sarah hadn't seen in years but had kept in touch with through social media and the occasional message.

"Sarah!" Emma exclaimed, crossing the room to greet her. She wrapped her arms around Sarah in a hug, her energy infectious. "I can't believe you're really here!"

Sarah laughed, feeling the tension in her shoulders loosen. Emma's enthusiasm was a welcome relief. "It's been too long, hasn't it?"

"It really has. I've missed you so much," Emma replied, stepping back and giving Sarah a look that conveyed her excitement. "I know things have changed, but it's still nice to be together again."

As the rest of the group filtered in, the atmosphere in the café began to shift. The initial awkwardness was slowly giving way to the comfort of familiarity, as if the group was remembering who they had been and, in turn, who they could still be together. There was a sense of unspoken understanding in the air, a realization that though time had passed, the bond they once shared was still there, lingering beneath the surface.

Some friends were eager to reconnect, diving straight into conversation with ease. Others, like Sarah, were more reserved, unsure of how to navigate the new dynamic. The group had changed, and though the foundation of their friendship remained, there was a subtle shift in the way they interacted.

Tom and Emma were chatting with one another, laughing about a shared memory from college, while Jason and a few others caught up on life since graduation. Sarah felt a twinge of nostalgia as she listened to their voices, the memories of late nights and endless conversations rushing back.

But she couldn't help but notice the gaps in the conversation. The moments where silence lingered, where old jokes and familiar stories didn't quite fit anymore. It wasn't that they had lost touch—it was just that they had all moved on, and the space between them was now filled with the weight of years spent apart.

As the group continued to chat, Sarah found herself drifting in and out of conversations. She felt a little disconnected, like an outsider in her own past. She had changed, yes, but so had everyone else. She could see it in the way they spoke, the way they held themselves. They were no longer the carefree students they had once been; they were adults, with adult lives and responsibilities.

The realization hit her suddenly, and she couldn't ignore it. The group had moved on, and so had she. The reunion, as much as she had hoped it would be a return to the past, was something entirely different. It was a chance to connect again, yes, but it was also a moment to acknowledge the distance that had grown between them all. The past was just that—the past. They couldn't go back, no matter how much they might want to.

But that didn't mean they couldn't move forward. The thought lingered in her mind, and she couldn't shake the feeling that this reunion wasn't about rediscovering who they had been—it was about discovering who they could be now. Together, yes, but also individually. They had all changed, but maybe that was okay.

As Sarah glanced around at her friends, she felt a flicker of hope. Maybe they could still find something meaningful in the new versions of themselves. Maybe the awkwardness and the changes were just part of the journey.

As the morning wore on, the café became filled with chatter and laughter, the kind of reunion banter that had always been a hallmark of their group. The old stories resurfaced, and memories long buried bubbled to the surface. But beneath the laughter, Sarah could sense a subtle tension hanging in the air. It wasn't loud or overt, but it was there, lurking just beneath the surface of the conversations.

She caught a glimpse of Tom as he cracked a joke about their old college days, his voice light and playful. But there was something in his eyes—a flicker of something more guarded, more distant. Sarah had known Tom long enough to recognize that look. It was the look of someone who had changed, but didn't quite know how to show it. He wasn't the carefree, rebellious friend he had once been. No, that person was long gone. The man sitting across from her was a version of Tom that was still learning how to fit into the life he had carved out for himself.

Her gaze shifted to Jason, who was talking animatedly with Emma, a grin on his face. But Sarah noticed how his eyes darted over to her every now and then, as though checking to see how she was doing. His nervous energy was almost palpable. Jason had always been the life of the party—the glue that kept everyone together.

But today, he seemed uncertain, as though he wasn't sure how to lead them all back to that familiar place.

And then there was Emma. Emma, who had always been the one to smooth over any discomfort, who was eager to pull everyone back into the fold. Sarah could see the effort Emma was putting into making the reunion feel like old times. But there was a weariness in her eyes now, an acknowledgment that maybe the friendships they once shared couldn't be rekindled with the same ease. She had changed, just like the rest of them.

As the morning stretched into afternoon, Sarah noticed that the group seemed to divide naturally into smaller clusters. The conversations that once flowed seamlessly now felt stilted and awkward, as if everyone was walking around unspoken rules—rules they hadn't discussed, but that had silently emerged as the years had passed.

Sarah was sitting with Jason and Emma when she overheard a conversation from across the table. It was between Tom and one of their other old friends, Ben, who had been the quieter member of their group. Ben was discussing his latest career move, a new position he had taken up at a company in a different city. As he spoke, Sarah caught a few phrases that made her heart sink.

"I just feel like I'm in a different place now, you know?" Ben was saying, his voice low but clear. "I've moved on from the whole college mentality. I don't really connect with that version of myself anymore."

Tom nodded, but Sarah could see the discomfort in his posture. "Yeah," Tom replied, though his tone was guarded. "I get that. It's like... we've all outgrown that part of our lives. But, I don't know... Sometimes I feel like it wasn't just the lifestyle we outgrew. It's the people too."

Sarah's heart skipped a beat. She didn't know if Tom was talking about her, or about the group in general, but the implication hung heavy in the air. The past was a place they had all left behind, but had they also left behind the people who had once been their closest companions?

The words struck a chord deep inside Sarah. She felt the weight of the years that had separated them all, the moments when life had moved on while they had stood still in different corners of the world. Had they really outgrown each other? Was that what was happening now, as they sat together, trying to revive a part of themselves that no longer fit?

The doubts crept in slowly, insidiously. Maybe Tom was right. Maybe the version of themselves that had once been so effortless—so full of laughter and hope—was gone for good. Maybe there was no going back, no matter how much they tried to force it.

Her thoughts were interrupted when Emma leaned in, nudging Sarah gently. "Hey, you okay?" she asked, her voice soft and concerned.

Sarah nodded, a tight smile crossing her lips. "Yeah, I'm fine. Just... thinking."

Emma studied her for a moment, her eyes narrowing slightly. "You don't look fine. You look like you're miles away."

"I guess I am," Sarah said, her voice tinged with a sense of resignation. "It's just... strange, you know? How different everything feels. How different we all feel."

Emma's gaze softened, and she leaned back in her chair, crossing her arms as she thought for a moment. "I get it," she said finally. "We've all changed. And I think we're all still trying to figure out what that means. But Sarah, don't think for a second that just because we're not the same people we were before means we can't still have something real. You don't just lose that kind of connection."

Sarah met Emma's gaze, her heart aching at the sincerity in her voice. She wanted to believe Emma, wanted to believe that the ties between them could survive the distance that time had put between them. But the doubt still lingered, creeping into the corners of her mind. The group was here, yes, but was it the same group? Was she still part of it, or was she just an observer of something that had long since passed?

Later in the afternoon, the group made plans to go for a walk around the town. The weather was still perfect, and it felt like the right thing to do—to get outside, to reconnect with the town that had once been their home. As they walked together, the awkwardness between them became more apparent. Some friends stuck close together, while others wandered off, lost in their own thoughts.

Sarah walked beside Jason, the two of them falling into a quiet rhythm. The town had changed, she realized, as they passed familiar streets and buildings. The old diner was gone, replaced by a sleek coffee shop, and the park where they had spent countless afternoons was now full of new developments. The world around them was moving forward, evolving, while they remained trapped in the idea of who they once were.

"So," Jason said, breaking the silence, "how do you feel about all this? I mean, about the reunion. The group. Us."

Sarah hesitated, unsure of how to answer. How could she explain the mess of emotions swirling inside her? "I don't know," she said finally. "It's just... harder than

I thought it would be. I thought coming back here would make everything feel right again. But it feels like we're all trying to fit into a mold that's no longer ours."

Jason nodded, his expression thoughtful. "I get that. It's like we're all looking for something that doesn't exist anymore. I think that's why I was so hesitant to do this. But now, I think I just wanted to see if there was still something here, something worth holding onto."

"I don't know if it's about holding onto the past," Sarah said softly. "Maybe it's about figuring out what's left, what we can build now."

As the group continued their walk, Sarah found herself watching her friends more closely. The tension was still there, the distance between them all palpable, but there were also moments—small moments—where the old dynamic resurfaced. Laughter over an inside joke, a shared memory that made them all pause and smile. Those moments were fleeting, but they were real.

Maybe this wasn't about recreating the past. Maybe it was about finding new ways to connect, new ways to be present with each other. The old friendships had evolved, just as they had. But that didn't mean they were lost forever.

As the sun began to set, casting a golden hue over the town, Sarah felt a flicker of hope. Maybe they could find something new, something worth holding onto, in the space that had once been filled with shared experiences. Maybe the awkwardness and uncertainty were just the first steps in discovering how they could move forward—together, but also as individuals who had changed, who had grown, and who still had something worth sharing.

The sun had begun to dip lower in the sky, casting an orange glow across the town as Sarah and the group continued their walk. The quiet between them wasn't uncomfortable, but it was noticeable. Each step they took seemed to accentuate the changes that had occurred in their lives—the personal and emotional distance that had grown over the years.

Despite the tension, Sarah couldn't ignore the moments of connection that flickered through the air like sparks. Jason and Emma exchanged an inside joke, and the laughter that followed felt genuine, even if it was brief. Tom, usually the one to make dry comments, shared a look with Ben, and for a moment, Sarah saw the warmth of familiarity in their eyes. These small moments, these fleeting glimpses of what they had once shared, reminded her that despite the distance, something still lingered in the space between them.

As they walked down the main street of their hometown, Sarah found herself lagging behind the group, lost in her thoughts. The landscape was both familiar and foreign at once. The streets she had walked countless times in her youth now seemed distant, like a memory that didn't quite belong to her anymore. The store windows, the old church, the park—they had all been part of her past, but the past was no longer where she lived. The world around her had moved on, and she had moved with it, or so it seemed.

"Everything feels different, doesn't it?" Jason's voice broke through her reverie, and she looked up to see him walking beside her. He had slowed his pace to match hers, and there was something in his expression that made her realize he was feeling much of the same.

"It does," Sarah replied quietly. "I keep thinking about how everything used to be so simple. But now, it feels like there's this weight to everything, like we're all carrying pieces of lives we didn't have before."

Jason nodded. "Yeah. It's strange. I thought this reunion would bring things back to how they were, but maybe that's not the point. Maybe we're just supposed to see each other for who we are now, not who we were."

Sarah let his words sink in, the realization dawning on her. She had been holding on to the idea of returning to the past, to the familiar rhythms of their friendships. But as Jason had said, maybe that wasn't the goal. Maybe the goal was to accept who they had become, to see the changes not as obstacles but as opportunities for a new kind of connection.

The group reached the park by the river, the setting sun casting long shadows on the grass. It was peaceful here, and the quiet of the evening seemed to invite reflection. Sarah sat on a bench near the water, her hands resting in her lap as she gazed at the ripples in the river.

As the others wandered off to explore the area or find a spot to sit, Sarah couldn't help but feel a quiet sadness wash over her. This place, this park, had been the backdrop of so many memories—long summer days spent lying in the grass, talking about everything and nothing, making promises to each other that felt unbreakable. Back then, it had seemed like they would always be here, always be together.

But the years had stolen that certainty. They had all changed, and so had the way they saw each other. Sarah had spent so much time mourning what had been lost that she hadn't realized how much she had gained. She had built a life for herself outside of this group, a life that didn't rely on the past. And maybe, just maybe, that was enough. She didn't need to reclaim everything she had lost—she just needed to find a new way to be part of this group, to embrace the changes and the growth that had come with time.

As Sarah sat there, her thoughts wandering, she felt a presence beside her. It was Emma, who had quietly joined her on the bench without saying a word. They sat in silence for a few moments, each lost in their own thoughts, before Emma spoke.

"You're quiet tonight," Emma said softly, her gaze fixed on the water. "What's going on in that head of yours?"

Sarah sighed, the weight of the day pressing down on her. "I don't know, Emma. I keep thinking about how much has changed. How different we all are. It's hard to see us as the same people we were back then. And sometimes, I wonder if there's still a place for me in this group."

Emma turned to look at Sarah, her expression understanding but firm. "There's always a place for you, Sarah. It may not be the same as it was before, but that doesn't mean it's any less real. We've all changed. But we're still here, and that counts for something."

Sarah met her gaze, feeling the sincerity in Emma's words. She wanted to believe it, but the uncertainty still lingered. It wasn't just the changes in her friends—it was the changes in herself. She wasn't the same person she had been when they first met, and maybe that was what scared her the most.

"I just don't know if I can go back to being the person I was before," Sarah admitted. "I've changed, and I don't know if I can ever be that carefree again."

"You don't have to be," Emma replied, her voice steady. "You're still you. But maybe the person you are now is just as important as the one you were then. Don't measure your worth by who you were in the past. We're all different, and that's okay."

Sarah looked at Emma, feeling a flicker of hope. Maybe she had been holding on too tightly to who she used to be, afraid that letting go of that version of herself would mean losing her place in this group. But maybe it was time to let that version go and embrace who she had become. After all, her friends hadn't come here to relive the past—they had come here to see who she was now, just as she had come to see who they were.

As the evening continued, the group began to settle in for the night. The tension that had marked the beginning of the reunion had eased, replaced by a sense of tentative camaraderie. They gathered around the fire pit outside the cabin, the flames casting flickering shadows on their faces. Laughter filled the air once again, and this time, it felt less forced, more genuine.

Sarah found herself leaning into the conversation, laughing at an old joke, sharing a story from her life that felt just as relevant as the ones from the past. She wasn't the same person she had been, and neither were her friends. But that didn't mean they couldn't find a way to reconnect. They were all in this together, navigating the changes, trying to figure out how to move forward.

As the fire crackled and the stars filled the sky above them, Sarah realized that the reunion wasn't about going back to the past. It was about finding a way to create something new—something that acknowledged the changes they had all gone through, but still held on to the essence of the connections that had brought them together in the first place.

The group wasn't the same, and neither was she. But that didn't mean they couldn't still share something meaningful. After all, life was about change. And maybe, just maybe, this reunion was the beginning of something new.

Chapter III: Shared Memories

The evening settled into a comfortable routine as the group gathered around the fire pit outside the cabin. The crackling of the flames filled the air, accompanied by the soft sounds of the surrounding woods. The sun had fully set, leaving a velvet sky studded with stars. It was the perfect backdrop for what was about to unfold—an evening of stories, of remembering, and of revisiting the past.

Jason, always the one to stir up excitement, leaned forward in his chair, his face lit by the firelight. "Okay, okay, we've got to start this off right. We can't have a reunion without a round of good old reminiscing."

Emma, sitting beside him, rolled her eyes but couldn't hide the smile tugging at her lips. "You mean, rehashing all the embarrassing stuff from college?" she asked, raising an eyebrow. "Because I'm sure we've all forgotten about that."

"Oh, please, we're not THAT embarrassing," Jason said with mock indignation. "We're just LEGENDS in the making. I think we should start with our greatest hits— like the time we almost got caught by the cops for sneaking into that old warehouse by the lake."

The group chuckled, and Sarah couldn't help but feel a warmth spread through her chest. She remembered that night so vividly—how they had laughed in the face of danger, how nothing felt impossible back then. It had been one of those nights that had defined their friendship, the kind of night that made them feel invincible, like nothing could tear them apart.

As the fire crackled, the group began to share their stories, each one sparking new memories. Tom, who had been quiet for most of the evening, suddenly spoke up, his voice laced with nostalgia. "Remember the summer after graduation? We took that road trip up the coast. It was like we were all trying to outrun our futures, but we never talked about it."

Everyone fell silent for a moment, the weight of Tom's words hanging in the air. Sarah's mind immediately drifted back to that summer. It had been the last summer before everything changed—the last summer before they all went their separate ways. They had piled into a car and driven up the coast, chasing sunsets and freedom, all the while avoiding the inevitable questions about their futures. They had pretended, just for a little while, that they could hold onto their youth forever.

"That was the best summer," Emma said softly, her eyes distant as she relived the memories. "We didn't have a care in the world, not a single one. Just us, the open road, and the music blasting. I swear, that trip felt like it lasted a lifetime."

But as the laughter faded, there was an undertone of something more somber. The road trip had been full of joy, yes, but it was also the beginning of the end, when they all knew their paths were about to diverge. Sarah remembered the unspoken tension between them, the way they had all clung to each other a little tighter as the end of their time together approached. It had been a time of unspoken fear, the fear of growing up, the fear of leaving behind the people who had once meant everything.

The flashback hit Sarah like a wave, carrying her back to that summer. She saw herself in the backseat of the old, beat-up car, the wind in her hair, the music blaring through the speakers. Jason was driving, his eyes glinting with excitement, while Tom sat shotgun, grinning as he told one of his usual stories. Emma, beside Sarah, was laughing, her carefree spirit infectious.

But there had been more than just fun on that trip. There had been the quiet moments when they all realized that life was moving on. Sarah remembered the look in Emma's eyes as she stared out the window one night, the way she had seemed so distant, even though she was physically there with them. It was as if Emma was already thinking about what would happen once they all went back to their respective lives. And Sarah had felt it too—the heaviness of knowing that the world they had created together was coming to an end.

"I think we all knew that summer was a goodbye of sorts," Sarah said, her voice breaking the silence. "Like we were trying to hold onto something that was already slipping away."

Jason turned to her, his expression softening. "Yeah, but we didn't know what to do with it, did we? We just pretended everything would be the same."

"But it wasn't, was it?" Sarah added, the realization sinking in. "It couldn't be. We all had different dreams, different futures. And somehow, we ended up here."

The words hung in the air for a moment, the truth of them settling over the group. The road trip had been a beautiful, fleeting escape, but it had also been the beginning of the end. None of them had been prepared for the distance that would grow between them, for the way their lives would pull them in different directions.

The group fell into a reflective silence. The weight of those memories lingered in the air, and it was clear that while the past had shaped their bond, it had also left its scars. As much as they wanted to return to the easy camaraderie they had once shared, there was no denying that things had changed. The shared experiences that had once felt unbreakable now seemed like fragile threads that were fraying with every passing year.

Emma broke the silence, her voice quieter than before. "I don't think we ever really talked about it, did we? How we were all moving in different directions, how scared we were about what came next."

Tom shifted uncomfortably in his seat, glancing at the others. "I don't think any of us wanted to face that. It was easier to just pretend like everything was fine."

"But we weren't fine," Sarah said, the words slipping out before she could stop them. "We were all pretending that things would stay the same, that the future wouldn't change anything. But it did. And I think that's when we started drifting apart."

There was an uncomfortable pause, the truth of Sarah's words hanging heavy in the air. The friends had never really discussed the tension they had all felt at the time—the growing realization that they couldn't hold onto each other forever. It had been easier to laugh, to make jokes, to create memories that would tie them together, but none of them had acknowledged the fear they all shared. The fear of losing each other.

As the fire crackled, the group's laughter faded, and a quieter atmosphere settled in. The memories that had once seemed so vivid, so perfect, now appeared more complicated in the light of reality. The road trip, the late-night talks, the moments of triumph and joy—those memories were still cherished, but they were tinged with the understanding that not everything had been as carefree as it seemed.

Sarah found herself thinking about the difference between memory and reality. The way they had all idealized those moments, turned them into something flawless, when in truth, they had been filled with their own uncertainties, their own insecurities. The group had been closer than anything, but they had also been scared. They had known, on some level, that the end was coming, and they had tried to hold onto each other in whatever way they could, even as their futures began to take them in different directions.

And now, here they were, sitting around a fire, trying to reconnect with a version of themselves that no longer existed. Sarah realized that the past would always be there, but it couldn't be what defined them. The friendships they had once shared had been real, but so had the changes that had come with time. They couldn't go back, and they shouldn't try.

The fire flickered brightly as the group settled into a comfortable silence, each person lost in their own thoughts. The conversation had shifted from light-hearted banter to something deeper—something that had been waiting beneath the surface for years. Sarah could feel the weight of unspoken words filling the space, and she wasn't sure if anyone else felt it too, but the quiet felt heavier now. There was a subtle shift in the dynamic—a growing realization that the past they were reminiscing about had not been as perfect as they had once believed.

Jason finally broke the silence, his voice quieter than usual. "You know, I've always wondered... What if we had talked about all that? About how we were really feeling, about the future and everything? Do you think things would have turned out differently?"

The question hung in the air, unanswered. It was a question none of them had dared ask back then, at least not aloud. They had been too caught up in the thrill of youth, in the excitement of endless possibilities, to face the reality that things were about to change. They had been too afraid to confront the truth, too focused on holding onto the comfort of their shared experiences. Now, years later, they were forced to look at the truth of their past with clearer eyes.

"I don't think we were ready for it," Emma said, her voice soft and thoughtful. "I think we all knew, deep down, that everything was changing. But we didn't know how to face it. We didn't know how to hold on to each other and let go at the same time."

"Yeah," Tom added, his voice carrying a weight that hadn't been there earlier. "We all had our own stuff going on. We were all trying to figure things out in different ways. Maybe we didn't want to acknowledge how hard it would be to keep everything together."

Sarah nodded quietly, the truth of Tom's words settling heavily in her chest. They had all been trying to navigate their own futures, each person focused on their own path, unsure of how to reconcile that with the group they had formed. The friendships they had cherished were real, but the fear of change had kept them from addressing the inevitable.

The fire crackled again, and Sarah found herself staring into the flames. She remembered how they had all vowed that nothing would change, how they had promised to always stay close, to never let go of each other. But the promises had been made by younger versions of themselves, versions that had no idea what the future would hold. And now, they were forced to confront the reality that those promises had been made with the best of intentions, but they had been out of their control.

As the night wore on, the conversation turned toward some of the more painful memories—moments of heartbreak that had once felt like the end of the world, but now seemed like faded echoes in the distance. Sarah remembered the way their group had been tested during the tough times—the fights, the misunderstandings, the moments when it felt like everything was falling apart.

One memory stood out more than the others: the night Sarah had fought with Emma, over something trivial, or so it seemed in retrospect. The details had long been blurred by time, but the hurt, the raw emotion, was still fresh in Sarah's mind.

It had happened in their senior year of college, after they had all decided to stay in town for the summer. Sarah had been struggling with the idea of staying behind while everyone else seemed ready to move on. She had resented Emma for not understanding, for pushing her to let go of her fears and embrace the future. But the argument had escalated quickly, and before Sarah knew it, they were both shouting at each other, their words cutting deeper than they ever intended.

The next morning, after the storm had passed, Sarah found Emma sitting alone in the kitchen, her face red from crying, her eyes empty with hurt. Sarah had wanted to apologize, but the words had been trapped in her throat. She didn't know how to fix the damage, how to bridge the gap that had suddenly appeared between them. In the end, they had both quietly agreed to let it go, to pretend that everything was fine, even though the scar of that moment had never fully healed.

The flashback pulled Sarah back to that day—the tension thick in the air as she stood in front of Emma, her chest tight with the weight of words unspoken.

"I just don't get it, Sarah!" Emma had cried, her voice breaking. "Why can't you just let go? Why can't you see that we're all moving forward, that we can't keep living in this bubble?"

Sarah had felt a rush of heat in her cheeks, a mixture of frustration and hurt. "It's not that simple, Emma. Not everyone's ready to just... move on like you are. Some of us are still trying to figure out who we are, where we're going."

Emma had stepped back, shaking her head. "And you think we're not? You think we don't have our own fears? But we can't stay in this bubble forever, Sarah. We're all changing, and if you're not willing to change with us, then what's left?"

The words had struck harder than Sarah expected, and she had lashed out, not knowing how to defend herself, not knowing how to make Emma understand. The anger and frustration had built to a point where neither of them could hear each other anymore. And in the end, they had walked away from that argument, each one retreating into their own space, unwilling to acknowledge how much they had hurt each other.

Now, years later, as Sarah sat by the fire, she realized that the fight had been more than just a disagreement—it had been a symptom of something deeper. It had been their fear of change, their inability to face the reality that their lives were shifting in ways they couldn't control. They had been young and naïve, thinking that they could hold onto everything forever.

But they couldn't. No one could.

As the memories of that fight resurfaced, Sarah couldn't help but notice how the group was still navigating the same tensions. There were moments of joy, moments of connection, but there were also moments when it felt like the weight of their past mistakes hung over them, unresolved and unaddressed.

Jason seemed to sense it too, his earlier enthusiasm now tempered with a more thoughtful expression. "You know, I think part of why we've all struggled with this reunion is because we're still carrying all that old baggage," he said, his voice more serious than before. "We never really dealt with the things that broke us apart. We never really talked about how we all felt when things changed."

"I think we were all too afraid to," Sarah admitted, her voice quiet. "Afraid that if we acknowledged how much we had hurt each other, it would make everything worse."

"And we didn't want to face the truth," Emma added softly, her eyes downcast. "That we couldn't be the same people we were before. That we couldn't hold onto the past."

The group fell silent, the weight of the conversation settling over them. It was clear that while the past had shaped their bond, it had also fractured it in ways they hadn't fully realized until now. The road trip, the summer after graduation, the arguments, the quiet moments of doubt—they had all been part of the same story, one they had tried to bury beneath layers of laughter and shared memories.

But the past couldn't be buried forever. And now, as they sat around the fire, they were forced to confront it, to face the reality of their relationships and the impact that time had had on them.

The quiet that followed their admission was heavy. Each of them, in their own way, was grappling with the realization that the friendships they had cherished were not immune to the complexities of time. It was clear now that the shared memories, the adventures, the inside jokes, all of them were layered with more than just joy. There were cracks in the foundation of their bond, cracks that had formed over the years but had never been addressed. Until now.

Jason broke the silence, his voice low but steady. "I think it's time we talk about the stuff we've been avoiding," he said. "We can sit here and laugh about the good times, but if we don't talk about the stuff that tore us apart, then what's the point? We can't move forward without facing it."

His words hung in the air like a challenge. Everyone sat a little straighter, the weight of what he was suggesting settling in. No one wanted to revisit the pain of the past, but they also knew it was the only way forward.

Sarah looked at Emma, who had been the one to initiate many of their past conversations but who now seemed to be retreating into herself. Emma met her gaze, and for a brief moment, Sarah saw the vulnerability in her eyes that had been hidden for so long. They had both grown, but they had also carried the weight of their unspoken words.

"I think we need to talk about the fight," Sarah said, her voice steady despite the rush of emotions that surged within her. "I know we've all avoided it for years, but it's still there, lingering between us. And if we're going to move on from this, we need to face it."

The fire crackled loudly in the silence that followed, and Sarah felt a knot tighten in her chest. She wasn't sure if she was ready to confront everything that had happened between them, but she knew it was the only way to reclaim what was left of their friendship.

As Sarah spoke, the group fell silent, each person lost in their thoughts. The past felt alive again, the memories of that night from so many years ago rushing to the surface. The night of the fight was as clear as if it had happened yesterday. She could remember the sharp edge to Emma's voice, the hurt in her eyes, the way they had both spoken words they hadn't meant but couldn't take back.

It had started innocuously enough—one of those small disagreements that, in the moment, felt like nothing but a passing storm. But it had escalated quickly, fueled by unspoken fears and frustrations. Emma had accused Sarah of holding onto the past, of not moving forward with the rest of them. And Sarah, who had been struggling to let go of the security they had once shared, had retaliated in anger, lashing out at Emma for what she perceived as abandonment.

"I'm just scared, okay?" Sarah had shouted, her voice trembling with emotion. "You're all moving on, and I'm just stuck here, holding onto something that's already slipping through my fingers."

But Emma hadn't understood. She had looked at Sarah as though she was betraying them all, as though holding on to the past was somehow a weakness.

"I'm not holding on to the past, Sarah!" Emma had yelled back, tears in her eyes. "I'm trying to make a future for myself. And you... you're stuck in a place where you're not letting yourself grow."

The words had cut deeper than either of them realized, and the argument spiraled from there. The fight wasn't just about that moment—it was about everything they hadn't said over the years, everything they had been too afraid to confront. They were both terrified of what the future would bring, but neither knew how to face it together.

The memory lingered in Sarah's mind, the hurt still raw, even after all these years. It was one of the few moments she wished she could take back, one of the few things she wished they had handled differently. But that was the nature of life, wasn't it? The things they didn't talk about always had a way of catching up with them.

"I wasn't ready to let go," Sarah said softly, her voice tinged with regret. "I wasn't ready to face that everything was changing. And I lashed out because of it. I hurt you, Emma. And I'm sorry."

Emma's expression softened, and for a moment, Sarah thought she might see the walls they had built between them start to crumble. But Emma said nothing at first. She simply looked at Sarah, as if weighing the words, the apology, and the years that had passed since then.

Finally, Emma spoke, her voice gentle but firm. "I know, Sarah. I know. And I'm sorry too. I was so focused on trying to make everything work for myself that I didn't see what you were going through. I didn't understand that you were struggling too. I thought if I just moved on, everyone else would too."

There it was—the admission that had been waiting to be said. The realization that they had both been caught in the same struggle, each one trying to find their way in the world while simultaneously holding on to something that was slipping away. The world they had created together had changed, and neither of them had known how to navigate that change.

"I think we all wanted to hold on," Tom added quietly from across the circle. "We were afraid of what would happen if we let go, and so we just kept pretending everything was fine. But none of us were fine. We were all scared, and we didn't know how to admit it."

His words were simple but resonated with everyone around the fire. There had been fear—fear of the unknown, fear of change, fear of losing what had once felt like the only certain thing in their lives. And they had all responded to that fear in different ways.

As the night wore on, the group continued to talk—really talk—about the things that had once been left unsaid. They acknowledged their shared fears, their struggles, and the way they had each tried to carry the weight of their futures alone, without leaning on each other as they once had.

The fire burned brightly, casting flickering shadows over their faces, but there was something different in the air now. The tension that had once dominated their conversations was slowly being replaced by a sense of understanding—a mutual recognition of the pain they had caused each other, but also the desire to heal, to move forward.

"I think we've all changed," Sarah said softly, looking around at her friends. "And that's okay. It's just... we can't keep holding on to the way things were. We have to accept who we are now."

Emma smiled, a soft and sincere expression. "Yeah, we can't live in the past forever. But that doesn't mean we can't still be there for each other. We've all grown, but we're still here. And that counts for something."

The group sat in quiet reflection, the weight of the past finally easing, replaced by the hope that, despite everything, they could find a way forward together. It wouldn't be the same as it had been. But that was okay.

What mattered now was what they chose to do with the future.

Chapter IV: Unfinished Business

The night had been a gentle unraveling of the past. The group had shared memories, laughed, and for the first time in years, allowed themselves to confront the things they had hidden away. But as the fire began to die down, and the quiet settled over the group, Sarah could feel the shift—something was coming, something that would alter the fragile peace they had started to build.

They had been talking in circles, skirting around the deeper issues that still simmered beneath the surface. Even though they had addressed the pain of the past, there was something more—something that none of them had wanted to acknowledge for fear of what it might mean.

As the group began to stand and stretch, preparing to retire for the night, Jason, who had been quiet for much of the evening, leaned forward. His voice was softer now, but there was a seriousness to it that made Sarah's stomach tighten.

"I've been thinking," he began, his gaze shifting between the others. "About something that's been bothering me for a long time."

The words immediately sent a ripple of tension through the group. Sarah froze, her heart skipping a beat. She knew—instinctively—that whatever Jason was about to say, it wasn't going to be easy.

Emma turned her head, her expression guarded. "What do you mean?" she asked carefully.

Jason hesitated, looking down at the fire, his face partially illuminated by the dying embers. "It's about... something that happened before we all lost touch. Something I've carried with me for a long time. And it's time to address it."

The words hung in the air, and for a moment, Sarah felt a sense of dread sweep over her. She had no idea where Jason was going with this, but she knew it couldn't be anything good. There was a discomfort in the way the others shifted in their seats, as though they, too, could feel the weight of the conversation before it had even begun.

"I'm just going to say it," Jason said, finally looking up. His voice was steady, but there was a rawness to it that made Sarah's heart pound in her chest. "A while ago, I... I made a choice. And I didn't think it would come back to bite me, but it has. And I need to say it."

There was a long pause before he continued, and Sarah could feel the air around them grow thicker with tension. It was as though everyone was holding their breath, waiting for the words they weren't sure they wanted to hear.

"You all remember that summer," Jason said, his voice quieter now. "The summer after graduation. After the road trip. There was... something between me and someone in this group. And it's something I should have addressed back then, but I didn't. I didn't think it would matter, but now I know that it did."

Sarah's mind raced. Her gaze flicked around the group, landing on Emma, who was watching Jason with a mix of confusion and something else—something Sarah couldn't quite read. Emma had been the closest to Jason during those years, and Sarah couldn't help but wonder if this revelation had something to do with her.

"I don't know why I never spoke up about it," Jason continued, his voice thickening with emotion. "But I... I kissed someone. And I didn't tell anyone. I didn't tell Emma, and I didn't tell anyone else because I was afraid. I was afraid of what it would do to the group, and I was afraid of how it would change everything. And I'm sorry. I should've told you, but I didn't."

A heavy silence settled over the group, and Sarah could barely breathe. She looked at Emma, whose face had gone pale, her hands tightening around the edge of her seat. For a moment, it was as if the world around them had come to a standstill.

Finally, Emma spoke, her voice shaking with emotion. "Who?" she asked, her words barely above a whisper.

Jason met her gaze, his eyes filled with guilt and regret. "It was... it was you, Emma. I kissed you that night at the party, after we all said goodbye. And I never told you, never told anyone. I just... I couldn't."

The words hung in the air like an explosion, sending shockwaves through the group. Sarah's heart ached at the hurt she could see in Emma's eyes, but there was also something else—something deeper. Emma was hurt, but there was more than just betrayal. There was a sense of confusion, a sense of being let down by the one person who had always been her closest friend.

Emma stood up abruptly, her chair scraping loudly against the stone beneath them. Her face was a mixture of shock, anger, and disbelief. "Why? Why didn't you say something?" she asked, her voice tight with emotion. "Why didn't you tell me, Jason? You just let it go, like it didn't matter?"

Jason stood up as well, his hands raised slightly in a gesture of apology. "I didn't know how to tell you. I didn't know how to explain it. I didn't want to hurt you, and I didn't want to ruin what we had as friends. But I should've. I should've been honest."

The room was heavy with the weight of his words, and the silence that followed was suffocating. Sarah watched, her heart torn between the two of them. She knew Jason's guilt was real, but she could also see the deep hurt in Emma's eyes—the betrayal she must have felt, not just from Jason, but from the fact that this secret had been kept for so long, hidden away while they all pretended like everything was fine.

"You don't get it, do you?" Emma said, her voice trembling. "You can't just do something like that, and then act like it didn't happen. You can't just kiss me and keep it a secret and expect me to be okay with it. You don't get to choose when to tell me the truth, Jason. I had a right to know."

Jason lowered his gaze, his hands clenched at his sides. "I know," he said, his voice barely above a whisper. "And I'm so sorry. I was selfish, and I didn't think about how it would affect you. I should've been honest from the start. But I was scared—scared of what it would do to everything."

The tension in the air was palpable, and for a moment, it felt like the group had been torn in two. Sarah could see that Tom and Ben were trying to process everything, but they were largely silent, unsure of how to intervene. The conversation had become personal, too personal for any of them to step in without making things worse.

Sarah could feel the weight of the situation pressing down on her. Jason's confession had cracked something open that they hadn't even known was there, and now they were forced to confront it. Emma's pain, Jason's guilt, the group's discomfort—it all mixed into a storm of emotion that none of them were prepared for.

"Emma, I... I never meant to hurt you," Jason said, his voice low with shame. "I just didn't know how to deal with it. And now, I see how wrong I was. I understand if you can't forgive me, but I need you to know that I've carried this around for so long, and it's eating me up inside."

Emma turned away from him, her back stiff as she walked a few steps toward the edge of the group. "I don't know what to say, Jason. I don't know if I can forgive you for this. You kept something this big from me, and I don't even know why."

Sarah could feel the shift in the air as Emma's words hung in the space between them. The unresolved issue of betrayal had come to light, and now the group had no choice but to face the discomfort, the vulnerability, and the conflict that had been simmering for years. They had all hoped that this reunion would be a healing moment, a return to simpler times, but now it felt like the past was far from being resolved. It was just beginning.

The moments after Jason's confession were filled with a tension that no one could ignore. The once-comfortable fire pit, now dim with the fading embers, seemed to reflect the emotional distance that had suddenly stretched between them. Sarah's heart pounded as she watched Emma struggle with the revelation. Jason stood with his shoulders hunched, like a man awaiting judgment, while the rest of the group remained unnervingly silent.

The air was thick with unspoken words. Sarah felt caught in the middle, uncertain whether she should intervene or allow Emma the space to process what had just been said. She glanced at Tom and Ben, hoping one of them would step forward, but they seemed just as hesitant as she was. It was clear that this wasn't something they could easily resolve.

Emma, her back still turned to the group, took in a shaky breath. The sound of her exhale was enough to break the silence. She turned slowly to face Jason, her eyes brimming with hurt, but also something else—something deeper.

"I need to ask you something, Jason," Emma said, her voice shaking but steady. "Why didn't you ever tell me? Why did you let me live with the idea that everything was fine, when you were keeping something like that from me?"

Jason swallowed hard, his eyes pleading for understanding. "I didn't know how to tell you, Emma. I was afraid of ruining everything. I thought that if I told you, it would break something we had—something I wasn't ready to lose."

Emma's face darkened. "And you thought I wouldn't have wanted to know?" she asked, her voice rising with a mixture of disbelief and anger. "You didn't think I had a right to be part of the truth?"

"I was selfish," Jason admitted, his voice raw. "I didn't think it through. And I should've. But I was scared. And now it's too late, and I've hurt you."

The words that followed from Emma were not ones Sarah was expecting. "I think I understand why you did it," Emma said, her voice softening just a bit. "I mean,

I was there too, in my own way. We were all holding on to things, pretending everything was okay when it wasn't. I didn't know how to handle the idea of things changing either. But keeping that from me... it's not just a mistake. It's a betrayal. And it hurts."

Jason closed his eyes briefly, as if the weight of her words were too much to bear. "I know. And I'm sorry, Emma. I can't take it back. I can't undo it. I should've been better. But I'll carry that regret for the rest of my life."

Emma stood there, her arms crossed tightly, processing his words. It was clear that she wasn't ready to forgive him—not yet. The trust between them had been shattered, and that wasn't something that could be repaired in a moment, or even in a day.

Tom finally stood up, his voice cutting through the thick tension. "We're all carrying some kind of burden here," he said, looking between the two of them. "Jason's not the only one who's made mistakes. We all have our part in this. But I think it's time we stop pretending that everything's okay. If we're going to move forward, we have to stop avoiding the real issues."

Ben, who had been silent up until now, nodded in agreement. "Tom's right. We've all been walking around with these unfinished pieces, and it's time we faced them. If we don't, we're just going to keep repeating the same mistakes."

The words hit Sarah hard, and for the first time that evening, she realized that the issue between Jason and Emma was only one piece of a much larger puzzle. The group had been avoiding the deeper, unresolved issues for far too long. And now they had no choice but to face them.

As the conversation shifted, Sarah felt the weight of her own unfinished business. She had been quiet up until this point, caught between the tension between Jason and Emma, and her own unresolved feelings. But something in the way Tom and Ben spoke made her realize that this wasn't just about Jason and Emma's betrayal. It was about all of them, about the things they had each left unsaid and the distance they had allowed to grow between them.

She couldn't hold back any longer. "I think we all need to face the truth," Sarah said quietly, her voice trembling slightly. "We've all been hiding behind our own fears—fears of losing each other, fears of being alone. And that's why we never talked about the things that hurt us. But now it's tearing us apart."

Jason looked up at her, his eyes filled with gratitude for her honesty, while Emma's gaze softened, acknowledging the truth in Sarah's words. It wasn't just about what Jason had done; it was about the way they had all allowed their fears to dictate their actions, how they had kept their emotions bottled up instead of confronting them.

"I'm scared, you know?" Sarah continued, her words flowing more freely now. "I'm scared that everything we've built is falling apart because we didn't deal with the tough stuff. I was so afraid of losing the bond we had that I kept pretending like things were fine. But they're not. We've all changed. And it's okay that we've changed, but we need to be honest about it."

The group fell silent again, but this time, there was a shift in the air—a shift towards understanding, towards a collective realization that they had been running from the very things that could heal them.

Emma stepped forward, her expression softening as she faced Jason. "I don't know how long it's going to take for me to forgive you, Jason," she said, her voice quieter now, more vulnerable. "But I don't want to keep carrying this anger. I want to be able to trust you again. I just don't know how yet."

Jason nodded, a silent agreement hanging in the air. "I understand. I'm not asking you to forgive me right now. But I want to do whatever it takes to make it right."

Sarah could see the sincerity in Jason's eyes, and she could feel the weight of the vulnerability that was now present in the group. It wasn't just about the past mistakes—it was about opening up, about being honest with each other, and about admitting that they were all carrying burdens they couldn't face alone.

"I think we've all been too afraid of facing the truth," Tom said, his voice steady but filled with emotion. "We didn't want to admit that we've all hurt each other, that we've all made mistakes. But we're here, right now, trying to fix it. And that's the first step."

Ben looked around at the group, his expression thoughtful. "It's not going to be easy. And it's not going to happen overnight. But if we can't be honest with each other, then what's the point of trying to fix it at all?"

The words echoed in Sarah's mind, and she realized how true they were. It wasn't going to be easy. There were still so many things left unsaid, so many feelings left unspoken. But for the first time in a long time, she felt like there was hope—that they could work through the unfinished business they had been avoiding.

The conversation lingered in the air like a fragile thread, each of them aware that the words spoken had unraveled something profound—something that could not be easily fixed. Sarah felt both exhausted and relieved, like they had just taken the first steps in addressing years of unspoken hurt. But as they sat in the dim light of the fire, the weight of their vulnerability was not lost on her. This wasn't a resolution—it was the beginning of a long, difficult journey.

"Maybe this is a good thing," Emma said quietly, breaking the silence. Her voice was steady but still raw, like she was carefully choosing her words. "Maybe all these things we've been avoiding are the things that will help us heal. But I can't just pretend like everything is fine, not after all this."

Jason nodded solemnly, his eyes filled with a mix of regret and determination. "I get that. I don't want you to just forgive me and move on. That's not fair to you. But I'm here. And I'll do whatever it takes to prove that I'm not the same person who kept that secret."

The fire crackled softly, the flames casting flickering shadows over their faces, but the tension was still palpable. There was so much left unspoken, so much still unresolved, and Sarah knew that this moment, however raw, was only the start of a much harder conversation.

"It's going to take time," Sarah said, her voice steady but full of emotion. "We can't just pretend like everything's okay. I don't know if we'll ever go back to the way things were, but maybe that's okay. Maybe we don't have to. But we have to be honest with each other now."

Tom looked up from the fire, his expression thoughtful. "Honesty isn't easy. It wasn't just Jason who kept things from others. We've all been hiding things, even from ourselves. And now, we have to face it. All of it."

Ben, who had been unusually quiet, cleared his throat. "It's not going to be comfortable, but maybe that's what we need. To be honest about everything—about the things that hurt, the things that we've buried. If we're ever going to move forward, we have to get through this together."

The words hit Sarah deeply, and she could feel the weight of their collective understanding. The unfinished business wasn't just about Jason's secret; it was about everything they had kept from each other over the years—the lies they had told themselves, the fear of losing each other, the unresolved conflicts that had been swept under the rug in an attempt to preserve a fragile sense of peace.

The group sat in silence for a long moment, each person reflecting on the truth of what had been said. There was a sense of discomfort, of rawness, that hung in the air, but there was also something else—something that felt like hope. They had started to peel away the layers of their shared history, and though the process was painful, it was also necessary.

Jason, breaking the silence, spoke again. "I think we've been afraid to face what's really inside. But I don't want to be afraid anymore. I don't want to carry this guilt around. I don't want to pretend like everything's fine if it's not. I'm not perfect, and I don't expect anyone to forgive me right away, but I want to work through this. If you'll let me."

Emma, still standing off to the side, looked at him for a long moment. Her gaze was searching, as though she was weighing his sincerity, but after what felt like an eternity, she nodded slowly. "I'm not ready to say I forgive you, Jason. But... I'm willing to try. To see if we can rebuild something. I don't know what that looks like, but I don't want to let this destroy everything. Not yet."

Sarah watched them, her heart heavy with the complexity of their situation. This wasn't an easy fix. The wounds they had all carried were too deep, too long unresolved. But in that moment, Sarah understood something vital: healing wasn't about erasing the past. It was about acknowledging it—acknowledging the hurt, the mistakes, and the fear—and choosing to face it together.

The fire flickered once more, casting long shadows over the group, and Sarah realized that this was the first real step they had taken toward healing. It wasn't perfect, it wasn't without pain, but it was a start. And that was all they could ask for.

"I think we've all been afraid of facing the truth," Sarah said softly, glancing around at the others. "Afraid of what it might mean, afraid of what it might cost. But we can't keep living like this—always pretending, always hiding. We need to be vulnerable, even when it scares us."

Ben nodded in agreement. "I think that's the only way we can move forward. If we're not honest with each other, then what's the point of even being here? What's the point of this reunion if we can't be real with each other?"

"I don't know if we'll ever get everything back to the way it was," Emma said, her voice still tentative, but more hopeful than before. "But maybe that's not what we need. Maybe we just need to figure out what comes next. And whatever that is, we need to be okay with it. Even if it's messy."

The group sat quietly for a moment, taking in Emma's words. There was a collective sense of vulnerability in the air—a recognition that the road ahead would not be easy, but that it was something they could face, together.

As the night wore on, the group continued to talk, but this time, there was a sense of openness, a willingness to face the things they had been avoiding. The stories of their pasts, the things they had kept hidden, slowly began to unfold. It wasn't a cathartic release all at once—it would take time—but the conversation had shifted. There was no longer an expectation that everything would go back to how it was before. Instead, they were beginning to understand that healing wasn't about turning back time—it was about moving forward with the truth, whatever that looked like.

As the fire burned low and the night grew colder, Sarah couldn't help but feel both exhausted and strangely lighter. The weight of years of unspoken words and unacknowledged pain hadn't disappeared, but the group had taken the first step in confronting it. There was still so much to navigate, so many emotions to work through, but for the first time in a long while, Sarah felt like the burden of silence had been lifted.

She looked at her friends, knowing that things would never be the same again—but also realizing that maybe that was okay. They had all changed, they had all grown, and now it was time to accept the new versions of each other. It wouldn't be easy. There would still be moments of discomfort, of doubt, of unresolved tension. But in the end, it was worth the effort.

Sarah took a deep breath, feeling the crisp night air fill her lungs. Whatever came next, they would face it together. And that, at least, was a start.

Chapter V: The Divisions

The fire had long since burned down to embers, the last traces of heat escaping into the cold night air. The group had spent hours talking, unraveling years of hidden emotions and unspoken truths. But as the conversation began to wind down, something shifted in the atmosphere. It wasn't obvious at first, just a subtle tension that no one could ignore. As the last of the wine bottles were emptied and the laughter began to fade, the group started to divide naturally into smaller groups.

It wasn't something anyone had consciously decided to do—it simply happened. The group of friends that had once been inseparable began to splinter, each person gravitating toward someone they had been closest to in the past. Emma and Sarah found themselves sitting together, exchanging a quiet glance that spoke volumes, while Jason and Tom stood by the fire, their conversation growing more animated as they reminisced about their old adventures.

Ben, who had largely remained quiet throughout the evening, slipped away toward the cabin. His silence was deafening, and Sarah noticed how he had been retreating more and more as the night progressed. It wasn't like him to be so withdrawn, but the unease between the group seemed to be weighing heavily on him.

And then there was Jason—he had always been the social one, the glue that held everyone together, but tonight, he seemed disconnected. His eyes flickered over to Emma, then to Sarah, before settling on Tom and Ben. It was clear that the emotional weight of the evening had begun to settle into a complicated mix of old alliances and unresolved tension.

As the smaller groups formed, Sarah couldn't ignore the palpable tension that had begun to take root. She and Emma sat on the edge of the cabin's porch, watching the others interact, but there was an uncomfortable feeling in the air—one that she hadn't expected. Emma, usually the peacemaker, was now quieter than Sarah had ever seen her. She had always been the one to bridge gaps, to soothe old wounds, but now, there was a visible wall between her and Jason, and Sarah could feel it.

Jason and Tom's conversation had taken a sharp turn when they started discussing old college rivalries—something that, in retrospect, had always been a source of friction between them. Sarah watched as Tom's face tightened, his earlier openness now replaced by the cool detachment that had always been his defense mechanism.

"Are we really going to do this now?" Sarah muttered under her breath, glancing at Emma, who was staring into the distance, seemingly lost in thought.

"I don't think we have a choice," Emma replied softly, her eyes narrowing as she observed Jason and Tom's heated exchange. "You can't undo years of competition and bitterness just because you're all sitting around a fire together."

Sarah nodded, her eyes drifting back to the two men. The old rivalry between Tom and Jason had been one of the quiet undercurrents of their friendship—a competition for dominance that, at the time, had felt like something harmless, a part of their dynamic. But now, after all these years, it seemed like something that could tear them apart again.

"I don't get it," Sarah said, her voice frustrated. "We've just had this big emotional moment where we're supposed to be confronting our past, but they're still holding onto this petty rivalry."

"It's not just petty," Emma replied. "This has been simmering under the surface for so long that it's impossible to ignore. Tom and Jason… they both want to be the one who's right, who's in control. But neither of them are willing to admit that they've both changed, that they've both grown."

Sarah was silent for a moment, watching the two men. "It's like no matter how much we try to reconnect, we're still stuck in the roles we used to play. It's like nothing's changed."

Emma sighed. "People don't just change overnight, Sarah. Some things stay with you, even after all these years. The best we can do is try to make peace with that."

As the night wore on, the group became more and more divided. It was subtle at first—a word here, a glance there—but soon it became apparent that each person was clinging to the same old alliances, the same old patterns. Sarah, Emma, and Tom stayed near the porch, while Jason, Ben, and Jason's old college friends gravitated toward the fire.

The distance between the groups was palpable. No one was arguing, no one was raising their voice, but the silence between them spoke volumes. Sarah found herself drifting between the groups, unsure of where she belonged. She felt the weight of the divide, the unease that now surrounded them like a thick fog.

Ben was the first to speak about it. He had stayed mostly to the periphery all night, his unease growing as the hours ticked by. "It's funny, isn't it?" Ben said, his voice quiet but sharp. "We all came here thinking we could go back to how things were. But we're not the same people anymore. And we're not just going to fall back into the same old rhythms. The truth is, we've grown apart."

His words landed with a quiet finality, and Sarah watched as the others looked up at him, a mixture of surprise and discomfort flashing across their faces. No one had been willing to say it aloud, but Ben had voiced the truth they had all been avoiding. The group was splitting, slowly but inevitably, into cliques. The emotional baggage they had been carrying was too heavy to ignore.

As the night deepened, Sarah found herself questioning the very thing she had been hoping for all evening—the idea of reconnecting with the past, of rekindling the friendships they had once shared. She had wanted to believe that time and distance could be overcome with a few heartfelt conversations. But now, in the quiet space between the groups, she realized just how much things had changed.

She turned to Emma, who was lost in thought, her eyes distant. "Do you think we can really go back to what we had?" Sarah asked quietly, the vulnerability of the question sinking in.

Emma looked at her for a moment before shaking her head. "I don't know," she said honestly. "I think we're trying to, but there's a part of me that knows it's never going to be the same. And maybe that's okay. Maybe we have to let go of what was and embrace what's left."

The words stung more than Sarah expected. She hadn't realized until that moment just how much she had been holding onto the idea of their old friendship. But Emma was right. They had all changed—some of them for the better, some for the worse—and trying to go back was only setting them up for disappointment.

As the night wore on, the groups grew more divided. Jason and Tom's rivalry continued to simmer, now mixed with unspoken resentment. Ben remained on the outskirts, his presence a quiet reminder that not everyone was comfortable with the tension. The laughter had faded, replaced by awkward pauses and uncomfortable glances.

Sarah stood up, her body tense with the realization that no matter how much they all tried to reconnect, something had been lost. Something they couldn't retrieve. The dynamic that once made their friendship so special—so effortless—was gone, replaced by old resentments, unspoken truths, and the awareness that they had all grown apart.

She walked to the edge of the cabin and stared out into the night. The sky was clear, the stars shining brightly above, but the peacefulness of the scene only highlighted the dissonance within the group. She didn't know what to do next. The group had been fractured for so long, and now, it seemed as though the cracks had finally begun to show.

Was it possible to heal what was broken? Or were they just delaying the inevitable?

The air was thick with unspoken words as the groups continued to split, each person retreating into their own corners. Sarah couldn't help but feel the weight of the emotional distance growing between them, and she began to question whether anything they had shared in the past could survive the present. What was left of their bond if the very foundations—trust, shared experience, and understanding—had started to crumble?

She looked over at Emma, who still seemed lost in her thoughts. The old warmth that had once been a natural part of their friendship was now buried beneath layers of uncertainty and hurt. They had spent so many years leaning on each other, but now, as time had passed, it felt like that reliance was no longer mutual. Sarah wanted to reach out, to close the distance, but she didn't know how. She wasn't even sure if Emma wanted her to.

At the fire, Jason and Tom were still arguing, their voices rising with every word. What had started as a casual conversation about old memories had quickly spiraled into a clash of egos, with neither one willing to back down. Ben, as always, remained quiet, his face a mixture of frustration and resignation. He had never been one to get involved in arguments, preferring instead to observe from the sidelines. But tonight, even his silence felt louder than ever.

"I'm not sure we're going to fix this," Sarah muttered to herself, her gaze focused on the flickering flames. "I don't know if there's enough left to fix."

Emma, still sitting beside her, glanced up at her with a small, sad smile. "I've been thinking the same thing," she confessed. "We've changed, Sarah. All of us. And no matter how hard we try to hold onto the past, it's slipping away."

"I just..." Sarah trailed off, her voice faltering. "I just don't know if I'm ready to let go of who we were. But maybe that's what we need to do. Maybe it's the only way forward."

Emma was silent for a moment, and Sarah could sense that her friend was still processing everything. The admission wasn't easy for either of them, but it felt necessary. They had spent so much time chasing the ghost of who they had been, and it was clear that the more they tried to revive it, the more it slipped through their fingers.

Just as Sarah was beginning to reconcile with the idea that the past could no longer define them, a sudden shout pierced the quiet night. Jason had snapped, his voice cutting through the tension like a blade.

"I'm sick of this!" he yelled, throwing his hands up in frustration. "Why is it always me? Why is it always my fault?"

The outburst caught everyone's attention, and for a moment, there was a stunned silence. Jason was standing, facing Tom with an intensity that was almost unnerving. Tom's face was red, his fists clenched, but it was clear that both of them were operating on pure emotion—old wounds resurfacing in a battle neither had wanted to fight.

Sarah stood up quickly, instinctively moving toward the center of the group. "Jason, stop!" she called out. "This isn't helping. We've been through enough tonight."

Jason didn't respond right away, his breathing heavy as he glared at Tom. Finally, he turned to Sarah, his eyes wild with frustration. "You don't get it, Sarah. You don't get what it's like to always be the one who holds everything together, the one who gets blamed for everything. I can't do it anymore."

Tom took a step forward, his voice low but firm. "We're not blaming you, Jason. You're the one who's been keeping things from us, and now we're all paying for it. You can't keep hiding behind that façade, pretending like everything's fine when it's not."

The words hit like a punch, and Jason flinched, the anger on his face replaced by something softer, something that looked suspiciously like guilt. But he didn't back down. "I've been trying to hold this damn group together, Tom. I'm the one who's been trying to fix everything, and it's never enough. You want the truth? Fine. We're all screwed up. We've all changed, and none of us are the people we used to be. We can't go back to what we had, no matter how hard we try."

The confession was raw, unfiltered, and it seemed to hang in the air, echoing the doubts that had been swirling around the group all evening. No one spoke for a long moment, the reality of his words settling over them all. They were all carrying burdens, all trying to navigate their changed relationships, and none of them knew how to fix it.

Sarah, still standing at the edge of the group, felt a sinking feeling in her chest. She had known for a long time that their relationships couldn't stay the same, that time had forced them to evolve, but hearing it out loud was different. The weight of their changes—their growing apart—was undeniable.

Emma spoke softly, breaking the silence that followed Jason's outburst. "We've all been pretending, haven't we? Pretending like things would just go back to the way they were. But they won't. And maybe that's okay."

Jason, his voice softer now, nodded slowly. "Yeah. Maybe it's okay." He turned to face the others, his expression more vulnerable than it had been all night. "But I don't know how to let go. I don't know how to stop pretending."

Tom, who had been quietly fuming, seemed to relax slightly, his posture less tense. "None of us do," he admitted. "We're all still figuring it out."

The group fell into an uneasy quiet, the weight of their collective truth hanging heavy in the air. They were all trying to move forward, trying to reconcile the past with the present, but the effort felt more difficult with each passing moment.

"I think we need to accept that we might never go back to what we were," Sarah said finally, her voice steady despite the heaviness in her chest. "But we can still be here for each other. We just need to figure out what that looks like."

There was a brief moment of silence before Emma nodded. "I agree. Maybe we don't go back. Maybe we just find a way to move forward, even if it's not easy. Even if it's messy."

Jason gave a short laugh, the sound bitter but tinged with understanding. "I think we've all learned the hard way that nothing's ever as simple as we want it to be."

The night wore on, the group slowly coming to terms with the reality of their situation. The divisions between them were clear, but in the quiet that followed the heated exchange, there was a sense of mutual recognition. They weren't the same people they had been, and they weren't sure if they could ever reclaim what they had once shared. But that didn't mean they couldn't try to build something new—something that acknowledged the complexities of their lives, the messiness of their emotions.

As the fire finally sputtered out and the cool night air settled in, Sarah couldn't help but feel a faint sense of hope. It wasn't a resolution, not by any means. There were still so many unresolved issues, so many things left unsaid. But for the first time that evening, there was an understanding that they couldn't keep running from the truth. They had to face it—and face each other—if they ever hoped to find a way forward.

As the night continued to unfold, the group's sense of division became undeniable. The conversations had become strained, the easy camaraderie that once flowed naturally now replaced by a quiet unease. It was as if the threads that had once tied them together were unraveling, slowly but surely. They had come together for this reunion with the hope of rediscovering the closeness they had once shared, but it was becoming increasingly clear that this was no simple task.

Sarah couldn't help but watch as Emma and Jason exchanged brief glances, their faces unreadable. The tension between them was palpable, and it was a tension that seemed to extend to the rest of the group. Jason, who had once been the bridge between them all, now seemed distant—almost like a stranger. His confession had cracked open something that couldn't easily be fixed, and though there was an unspoken desire to move forward, the past was not something they could simply sweep aside.

Ben, who had remained relatively quiet throughout the night, was the first to break the silence that had settled over the group. He had been sitting off to the side, watching the others interact with a growing sense of frustration. He hadn't spoken much during the emotional exchanges, but now, as the weight of the silence became too much to bear, he stood up.

"We're all pretending, aren't we?" Ben said, his voice cutting through the quiet like a knife. "We're pretending like everything is okay, like we can just pick up where we left off. But the truth is, we're not the same people we were. We've changed. And some of us are still holding onto things that no one else even knows about."

The words hung in the air, and for a moment, no one moved. The group had been avoiding the truth for so long, hoping that their shared memories would be enough to bridge the divide. But Ben's words brought that illusion crashing down. It wasn't enough. The past was no longer enough to hold them together.

As the conversation shifted once more, the group naturally divided further. Tom, who had been listening quietly to Ben's words, exchanged a knowing glance with Sarah. Their old alliance, built on mutual understanding and unspoken loyalty, felt like the only thing still holding any semblance of cohesion in the group. Yet even their bond had been tested tonight. The arguments, the confessions, and the confrontations had laid bare the fractures that had been growing for years.

Jason, who had been quieter since his outburst, stepped away from the fire. His eyes briefly met Sarah's, and for a moment, she thought he might approach her. But instead, he walked toward the cabin, disappearing into the shadows without a word. The sudden silence in his absence was almost deafening.

"I didn't expect this," Sarah said softly to Emma, who was still sitting by her side. "I thought we were past all the old issues. But it's like they've all resurfaced at once."

Emma, who had been visibly shaken by Jason's confession, nodded slowly. "It's not just the old issues, Sarah. It's that we've been avoiding them for so long. And now we're being forced to face everything at once. It's too much."

Sarah could feel the weight of Emma's words, and for the first time, she realized how true they were. The group had been avoiding their deeper conflicts for years, and now those unresolved tensions were coming to the surface. No one was left untouched by the pain of the past. The dynamics had shifted, the alliances had begun to fracture, and now they were all left to pick up the pieces.

As Sarah's thoughts wandered, her gaze fell on Jason, who was standing off by the edge of the cabin, looking up at the night sky. He seemed distant, lost in his own thoughts, but there was a deep sense of regret in his posture. Sarah had always seen Jason as the glue that held the group together, the one who could always lighten the mood, who could bring everyone together with a joke or a story. But tonight, the weight of his confession, of the hurt he had caused, had left him broken.

Emma noticed Sarah's gaze and followed it. "He's not the same person, is he?" she said quietly, almost as if talking to herself. "And I'm not sure I am either."

"No one is," Sarah replied, her voice thick with emotion. "We're all different now. I guess I just didn't expect the differences to be so... vast."

It wasn't just Jason who had changed. It was all of them. The past that had once bound them together now seemed like a distant memory, something they had outgrown without realizing it. Their shared experiences, the laughs, the inside jokes—they still had value, but the threads that once held them together had been loosened by time and distance.

The group had spent the entire evening trying to bridge the gaps between them, but with every conversation, every awkward silence, the divide only seemed to widen. The intimacy they once shared, the sense of belonging they had always felt in each other's presence, was slipping away. No matter how hard they tried to recapture it, the distance between them was now too great.

Ben, who had been standing quietly on the fringes of the group, suddenly spoke again, his voice quiet but firm. "We've all changed. And I don't know if that's a bad thing, but it is what it is. We're not going to be who we were, and we have to accept that."

The group turned toward him, and for the first time that night, the tension between them seemed to subside, if only for a brief moment. Ben's words were simple, but they carried an undeniable truth. They couldn't go back. They couldn't reclaim the past. They were all different people now, and maybe that was okay.

Sarah felt the truth of it settle deep within her. She had spent so much time trying to hold onto something that wasn't there anymore. She had clung to the idea of their old friendships, but the reality was that they had changed. They had all changed.

The fire was almost out now, the last few embers flickering in the cool night air. The group had drifted into a contemplative silence, each person processing the evening's events in their own way. The tensions were still there, still raw, but there was also a quiet understanding. They had been forced to confront the realities of their relationships, and though it was uncomfortable, it was also necessary.

As Sarah stood up and walked toward the cabin, she glanced back at the group. There was no resolution, no easy answers. But they had taken a step, a small but significant step, toward understanding that the past would not define them. They could move forward, not as the people they once were, but as the people they had become.

And maybe, just maybe, that was enough.

Chapter VI: A Moment of Clarity

The night had stretched on longer than anyone had anticipated. What had begun as a reunion filled with laughter, shared memories, and hopes for reconnection had slowly transformed into an uncomfortable reflection on the realities of their lives. The fire had burned down to nothing more than a collection of smoldering embers, and the group, now broken into smaller clusters, had grown quiet.

Sarah found herself sitting alone on the porch of the cabin, her legs tucked under her, staring out at the dark woods that surrounded them. The silence was thick, but in a way, it felt necessary. The constant chatter, the attempts to relive the past, had left her feeling more distant than ever. Now, in the stillness, she allowed herself a moment to breathe, to simply be.

The cool air of the night brushed against her skin, and for the first time in hours, she felt the weight of everything begin to lift. She was no longer surrounded by the noise of the group's discomfort, no longer trying to fit into the roles they had once assigned her. She was just Sarah—alone, in the quiet, with her thoughts.

She didn't know how long she had been sitting there before she felt the presence beside her. Emma, her silhouette outlined against the dim light of the porch, sat down next to Sarah without a word. There was something comforting about her silent companionship. Emma didn't need to speak; they both understood the weight of the evening without needing to discuss it.

The night was peaceful, save for the occasional rustling of leaves and the distant calls of animals in the forest. Sarah took a deep breath, allowing the stillness to fill her, and for the first time that evening, she allowed herself to truly reflect. What had she been hoping for when she arrived here? Was it really about rekindling the past, or was she simply looking for something familiar to cling to?

She had always believed that the past had a certain power over her, that the people she had once been closest to would always hold some kind of key to her happiness, her sense of self. But as the hours had unfolded, as the conversations turned into confrontations, she realized that maybe she had been wrong. Maybe the past was not something to return to—it was something to learn from, to grow from, and then to leave behind.

"Do you think we can ever really go back?" Sarah asked, her voice soft, almost a whisper in the still night air.

Emma was silent for a moment, as though contemplating the question herself. "I don't know," she finally said, her voice low. "I think part of me wants to go back, to have everything feel the way it used to. But I also know that we can't. We're not those people anymore, Sarah. And that's not necessarily a bad thing. We've all changed, and that change is part of who we are now."

Sarah nodded slowly, the truth of Emma's words settling in her chest. It was difficult to accept, but deep down, she knew it was the only way forward. The version of herself that had walked into the reunion, hoping for some kind of revival, was not the person she was meant to be. She had grown—just as they all had—and it was time to acknowledge that.

The past, with its old bonds and unresolved tensions, could not dictate her future. It was part of her, but it didn't define her. She was no longer the person she had been when she left this town years ago. She had created a life outside of the group, a life that had taken her in new directions, and now she had to ask herself: Did she really want to re-engage with this version of herself and her friends, or was it time to let go and move forward?

As the minutes ticked by, Sarah reflected on her own journey. She had spent so much of her life clinging to the idea of the past—of who she used to be, of who they all used to be. The thought of losing that connection had terrified her, but now, as she sat beside Emma, watching the night unfold around them, she realized that there was something liberating about accepting change.

She had built a life for herself—one that was different from the one she had imagined with this group of friends, but one that was still full of meaning. The relationships they had once shared were beautiful, but they were not meant to last forever. They were part of a chapter in her life, one that had taught her about love, loss, growth, and the power of letting go.

"You're right," Sarah said, her voice steady as she looked at Emma. "We've changed. And that's okay. Maybe we're not supposed to go back. Maybe we're supposed to move forward, even if it's hard."

Emma turned toward her, a soft smile tugging at her lips. "I think that's the first time you've said something like that all night."

Sarah couldn't help but laugh, the sound light and freeing. "I guess it took me a little while to get there."

They both sat in comfortable silence for a while longer, the quiet stretching between them as they each took in the significance of what had been said. Sarah wasn't sure what the future held for her and her old friends. She wasn't sure if they could ever truly reconcile everything that had changed. But one thing was certain: She had made peace with the fact that moving forward meant accepting the reality of their relationships—and her own.

The night sky above them seemed infinite, the stars twinkling in the distance like silent witnesses to the personal revelations unfolding below. Sarah closed her eyes for a moment, letting the cool air fill her lungs. The doubts and fears that had clouded her mind earlier were slowly dissipating, replaced by a sense of quiet clarity. She no longer needed to prove anything to anyone—not to herself, and certainly not to her friends. The person she had become was enough. The relationships she had built in her life, the ones that had evolved over time, were the ones that mattered now.

"We're not the same people anymore," Sarah said, her voice more confident than before. "And that's okay. I can't hold onto who we were. I just have to accept that. I think I'm ready to move on."

Emma nodded, her expression soft. "I think we all are. But it doesn't mean we have to forget what we shared. We just need to stop pretending that everything is how it used to be."

Sarah smiled, a genuine, peaceful smile that felt like a weight lifting from her shoulders. "Yeah. We're moving forward, together or apart, but we're moving forward."

The quiet stillness of the night wrapped around them like a blanket, and for the first time in a long while, Sarah felt at peace. There would always be things left unsaid, old wounds that might never fully heal. But she had made a decision. She was ready to leave behind the past and face the future. The group she had once known was gone, and she could either fight to bring it back or accept that it had served its purpose in her life.

As Sarah and Emma sat together, the weight of the evening's conversations slowly faded into the background. The quiet of the night was no longer heavy with doubt. It was a stillness filled with acceptance—a recognition that the future was uncertain, but that it was hers to shape.

And as the stars twinkled above, Sarah knew that whatever came next, she was ready for it.

As the night slowly gave way to the early hours of the morning, the air grew colder, but Sarah felt a sense of warmth inside her. The clarity she had found within herself seemed to settle like a gentle weight, neither heavy nor burdensome, but comforting in its quiet assurance. The world around her had remained unchanged, the stars still twinkling in the sky, the woods still whispering in the wind. But she was different. She had faced the uncertainty, the discomfort, and had come out the other side with an understanding that had been missing for far too long.

She stood up from the porch and stretched her legs, the cool breeze brushing against her face. Emma stood beside her, wordlessly offering her company as they both took in the calm of the morning. It felt strange—like a beginning that wasn't loud or dramatic, but one that was born from acceptance, from understanding.

Sarah turned to Emma, her voice quiet but resolute. "I think we both needed this. More than we realized."

Emma smiled softly, her eyes reflecting the same sense of quiet understanding. "I think so too. We were holding onto so much—the past, the expectations, the fear of letting go. But it's all part of growing up, isn't it? The letting go. The change."

"Yeah," Sarah agreed, her gaze drifting toward the horizon. "And we don't have to lose everything to move forward. We just have to accept that we're not the same people we were. That's okay."

For a moment, neither of them said anything. They stood side by side, each in their own thoughts, but connected by the mutual realization that the reunion—though difficult and emotionally charged—had led them to a moment of truth. It wasn't about reclaiming what was lost, but about finding peace with the changes they had undergone and the people they had become.

As Sarah stood there in the quiet of the early morning, she realized how much of her life she had spent chasing after versions of herself that no longer fit, clinging to relationships that had shifted, and trying to make things work that simply weren't meant to. The fear of change, the fear of being alone, had kept her trapped in the illusion that if she could just recreate the past, she could find happiness again.

But the truth was that happiness wasn't in recreating what was. It was in embracing what was yet to come.

The friendships they had once shared, the bonds that had shaped her, could still hold value, but they no longer defined her. Sarah had built a life of her own, one that didn't depend on old connections, on nostalgia, or on trying to relive a past that had already slipped through her fingers.

She looked at Emma, who was watching her with a quiet, knowing expression. "I think I'm finally ready to move on, Emma," Sarah said, the weight of her words finally sinking in. "I don't want to keep holding on to something that isn't real anymore. I want to move forward. And I want to do it with the people who are here now, not the people I wish were still here."

Emma gave a soft nod, her eyes filled with understanding. "It's hard, isn't it? Letting go. But I think you're right. We can't keep trying to resurrect what's already gone. The best thing we can do is embrace the future."

Sarah smiled, a small but genuine smile that felt lighter than she had in a long time. "Exactly. And I think... I think I'm finally okay with that."

As they stood there, the first light of dawn beginning to break over the horizon, Sarah felt an overwhelming sense of peace. The past was not something to be erased, nor was it something to cling to desperately. It had shaped her, and it had shaped the people around her, but it didn't hold power over her anymore.

She turned back toward the group, her gaze sweeping over them. Jason, Tom, and Ben were still gathered around the fire, their voices quieter now, but there was a tension that remained—one that was not easily dissolved. But for the first time that evening, Sarah didn't feel the need to fix anything. She didn't need to make everything right. She could move forward without trying to repair something that was beyond saving.

Emma gave her a sideways glance, a knowing look passing between them. "Are you ready to face them?" she asked gently.

Sarah took a deep breath and looked toward the group, the realization that she didn't have to fix the fractured pieces of the past washing over her like a wave of relief. "Yeah. I think I am. But I'm not going to pretend everything is okay anymore. I don't need to."

Emma nodded, a quiet smile tugging at her lips. "Neither do I."

As Sarah stepped back toward the group, she felt a sense of lightness in her chest. She was no longer the person who clung to the past, to the comfort of what had been. She was someone who had embraced change, who had found peace with the unknown, and who was ready to face whatever came next.

The path ahead was uncertain, but for the first time in a long time, that uncertainty felt like freedom.

As the sun continued to rise, the group gathered together in the warmth of the morning light. There were no more dramatic confessions, no more fights, no more unresolved tensions hanging in the air. The group was still fractured, still carrying the weight of their differences, but there was an understanding now, a mutual recognition that they had all changed, and that change was okay.

Jason, standing a little off to the side, caught Sarah's eye. He nodded at her, his expression softer than it had been the night before. The rivalry, the bitterness—those things were still there, but there was an acknowledgment now that they had all grown, had all changed. And maybe that was enough.

As Sarah looked around at her friends, she felt a quiet sense of resolution. It wasn't about fixing everything. It was about moving forward, accepting who they had become, and knowing that they had the power to create their own paths. The past would always be part of them, but it didn't need to define their future.

And as the group slowly began to pack up, preparing to go their separate ways, Sarah realized that she was no longer afraid of the future. She was ready to face it, with all of its uncertainties, with all of its changes, and with all of the lessons that had come from the past.

The morning light filtered softly through the trees, casting long shadows across the cabin and the group of friends who remained. The night had taken its toll on everyone, and there was a weariness in the air, but it was not an oppressive kind of exhaustion. It was the kind of tiredness that came from confronting the past, from facing uncomfortable truths, and from finally letting go of the things they could not control.

Sarah watched as the group began to pack up their belongings, the conversations quieter now, less charged with tension. The dynamic had shifted. They were no longer trying to force a return to what they had been. They were each coming to terms with who they had become, and in doing so, they were learning to navigate their relationships in a new way.

Emma was the first to break the silence as she started to gather her things, a quiet smile on her face. "It's strange, isn't it?" she said, looking at Sarah. "The way everything has shifted. But I think we're all better for it."

Sarah nodded, feeling a sense of peace in her chest. "Yeah. We're not the same people anymore, but maybe that's okay. Maybe it's time to let go of the idea that we can ever be who we once were."

Emma chuckled softly, a hint of sadness in her eyes. "It's hard to let go of that idea, though. We spent so many years trying to hold onto it. But you're right. We have to accept that things have changed."

As Sarah continued to watch the others, she felt a surge of gratitude. They had all been through so much, individually and together, and despite everything, they had made it this far. They had come together for a reunion that, at times, felt like a last-ditch effort to preserve something that was already slipping away. But in the end, they had faced the truth and found a way to move forward.

It was time to leave. There was no grand resolution, no sweeping gesture of reconciliation, but the group had reached an understanding. The bonds they had once shared had been tested, and while some might have been irreparably fractured, there was still room for new beginnings. They didn't need to cling to the past to move forward.

Sarah walked toward the car, her steps light but purposeful. She glanced over her shoulder at Emma, who was still quietly packing up her things. There was no need for words between them. They had both come to the same understanding. It was time to step into the future, to embrace the unknown, and to accept that the relationships they had once cherished would never be the same.

As Sarah reached the car, Jason caught her eye. For a moment, he seemed unsure, but then he nodded, a silent acknowledgment passing between them. It wasn't forgiveness, not yet, but it was the beginning of something new. He had taken the first step in admitting his mistakes, and though they still had a long way to go, it felt like a turning point.

"Goodbye, Sarah," Jason said quietly, his voice steady.

Sarah smiled, a small but genuine smile. "Goodbye, Jason."

The others began to gather their things, and the moment of parting seemed inevitable. There was no dramatic farewell, no promises of forever. Instead, there was just an understanding—an acknowledgment that they had all changed, and that maybe it was time to let go of the past and embrace the future, whatever it might hold.

As Sarah climbed into the car and started the engine, she felt a sense of peace wash over her. The future was uncertain, yes, but it was hers to shape. She didn't need the approval of the past to move forward. She didn't need to relive old memories or try to fix things that couldn't be fixed. She was ready to face whatever came next.

As she drove away from the cabin, the trees and familiar landscape began to fade into the distance. The roads she had once traveled with her friends seemed less significant now. The memories of the past, while valuable, no longer held the same weight they once did. Sarah had made peace with the idea that the future was not a place she could control, but a place she could embrace. And she was ready.

The silence in the car was comforting, and as Sarah drove, her thoughts turned inward. She had spent so much of her life trying to hold onto the past, to the people she had once been, to the group that had once been everything to her. But now, she knew that the future was hers to navigate on her own terms.

There were still things left unsaid, things left unresolved, but she didn't need to fix everything. She didn't need to tie up all the loose ends. Some things were just meant to be left behind, and the most important thing was to keep moving forward.

As she turned onto a new road, a sense of excitement bubbled within her. The journey ahead was unknown, filled with possibilities she hadn't yet imagined. And for the first time in a long time, she felt truly free.

The Confrontation

Chapter VII: Bitter Revelations

The evening had begun with an air of tentative peace. After the initial awkwardness of their reunion, the group had begun to settle into a quieter rhythm, each person retreating into their own thoughts, processing the emotions that had resurfaced after so many years. The fire had died down to a faint glow, and the group sat in clusters, their conversations more subdued than before.

But the calm was deceptive. Beneath the surface, old wounds festered, and cracks were beginning to show. The alcohol, which had been flowing freely throughout the night, was beginning to take its toll. The warmth it provided had loosened tongues and stirred up feelings long buried, setting the stage for a confrontation none of them had anticipated.

Sarah watched as Jason, his face flushed from the wine, leaned in toward Tom, who had been strangely quiet all evening. She had always been able to sense when something was wrong, and tonight, there was a tension between them that couldn't be ignored. The air had shifted, and Sarah could feel the storm brewing.

"I don't get it, man," Jason's voice cut through the murmur of the group. He was slurring slightly, but his tone was sharp, his frustration clear. "All this time, and you still haven't said a word about it. You've just been sitting there, acting like nothing happened."

Tom looked at him, his expression cold and unreadable. "Maybe I don't feel like rehashing everything right now, Jason," he replied, his voice tight. "Maybe I'm not in the mood to relive the same old shit."

Jason's eyes narrowed, and Sarah saw the muscles in his jaw tense. There was a storm in his eyes, something angry and unresolved. "It's not the same old shit, Tom. You were supposed to be my friend. You were supposed to have my back."

The words hung in the air like a challenge, and Sarah felt the shift in the atmosphere. The group had been tiptoeing around their pasts for hours, but now, with the alcohol working its way through their systems, the facade of civility was starting to crack. Jason had always been the one to keep things light, to defuse tension with a joke or a grin, but now, there was a rawness to his words that no one could ignore.

Tom took a deep breath, his eyes meeting Jason's with a quiet intensity. "You want to talk about it?" he asked, his voice low. "Fine. But don't act like you weren't part of the problem, too. Don't act like you didn't play a role in everything falling apart."

The words landed with a heaviness that shocked Sarah. There was something in Tom's gaze—something deep and unforgiving—that sent a ripple of unease through the group. She could see the other friends slowly turning toward them, sensing the shift in the dynamic. This was no longer just a casual conversation. It was a confrontation, and it was about to escalate.

Jason didn't back down. "Oh, so now you're going to blame me?" he spat, his voice rising. "That's rich, Tom. You've been sitting on your high horse for years, acting like you have all the answers. But you never said anything. You just let it all fall apart. You didn't even try to fix things. You just walked away."

The words hit like a slap, and Sarah could see the anger in Tom's eyes flare. He stood up suddenly, his chair scraping loudly against the floor. The group fell silent, the tension in the air thickening.

"Don't talk to me about walking away," Tom said, his voice cold. "You think you're the only one who had shit to deal with? You think I didn't want to fix things? But you made it impossible, Jason. You pushed everyone away with your bullshit, your games. You were always the center of attention, the one everyone flocked to. And when things got tough, when people needed you, where were you?"

Jason staggered slightly, his face reddening with rage. "You think I didn't have my own problems? You think I didn't have shit to deal with too? You don't know what it was like. You don't know what I was going through."

Tom's face twisted with a mix of frustration and hurt. "Maybe I didn't, but you never let anyone in. You pushed everyone away, and when we needed you the most, you weren't there."

The words hung in the air, and Sarah could feel the weight of them. She had never seen Tom so angry, so vulnerable. There was so much between them all—so much unsaid, so much that had been buried for too long.

The silence that followed was thick and suffocating. Sarah glanced around the group, her eyes meeting Emma's. Emma was sitting quietly, her face a mixture of concern and disbelief. She had always been the mediator, the one to step in and calm things down, but tonight, she seemed just as stunned as the rest of them.

Jason finally broke the silence, his voice quieter now but no less intense. "I never asked for your forgiveness,

Tom. I never wanted to be the person who let everyone down. But that's who I am. That's who I've always been."

Tom's expression softened, just slightly. "And you think that makes it okay? You think that excuses everything?"

Jason didn't answer right away. Instead, he took a long gulp from his glass, his eyes staring into the fire. "No," he said, his voice hollow. "It doesn't. But that's the reality of it. I messed up. And I know that. But you can't sit there and act like you were the perfect friend either, Tom."

The group was now fully engaged, the conversation spilling over into a confrontation that no one had been prepared for. Sarah felt a mix of discomfort and something else—something like relief. They had all been dancing around the truth for so long, pretending like everything was fine, but now it was out in the open. The bitterness, the anger, the hurt—they had all been simmering beneath the surface, and now they were spilling out with a force no one could control.

Tom took a step toward Jason, his face inches from his. "I never claimed to be perfect. But at least I didn't hide behind my bullshit and pretend like everything was okay. You could never just be honest with anyone, Jason. You couldn't even be honest with yourself."

Jason's fists clenched at his sides, but instead of lashing out physically, he took a step back, his eyes clouded with anger and regret. "You think I didn't know that? You think I didn't see what I was doing? But I couldn't fix it, Tom. I couldn't fix myself. And maybe I've been too scared to admit it. But I'm not the only one who's messed up."

The confession hung in the air, raw and heavy. Sarah could see the emotional toll it had taken on both of them. Jason was unraveling before her eyes, his facade cracking, revealing the pain and fear he had kept hidden for so long. And Tom, who had always been the more stoic of the group, was finally showing the cracks in his own armor.

It was painful, it was messy, but it was real. And for the first time in a long time, Sarah realized that this was the only way forward. They couldn't heal without facing the truth, without confronting the bitterness and resentment that had been festering between them.

The tension between Jason and Tom was palpable. The words that had been exchanged had ignited something deeper, something that no one had been prepared to confront. The group had gathered together, trying to reconnect, but now, in the midst of anger and frustration, it felt like everything they had once shared was unraveling, thread by thread.

"Maybe you're right," Jason said suddenly, his voice hoarse, "maybe I never faced up to what I was doing. But I did what I had to, man. I buried it all, and I buried it deep, so I wouldn't have to deal with it."

Tom crossed his arms, his expression unreadable. "And look where that got us. You can't keep running from yourself forever, Jason. Eventually, it all catches up to you."

The group was silent, watching them, unsure of whether to intervene. Emma looked at Sarah, her face pale, her mouth set in a tight line. She had always been the one to smooth things over, to ease tensions when they got too high, but tonight, it seemed like the rift between Jason and Tom was too deep, too old, to be fixed with words.

"Enough!" Ben's voice suddenly cut through the growing chaos, his tone sharp and commanding. He had been standing at the edge of the group, watching the confrontation unfold, and now, his patience seemed to have reached its breaking point. "This isn't helping. We're not getting anywhere by screaming at each other."

Jason turned to Ben, his eyes bloodshot and unfocused, as though he was trying to steady himself. "You don't understand, Ben. You didn't see it, you didn't live it. I didn't ask for any of this. I didn't ask for things to fall apart."

Ben took a step closer, his voice still steady but filled with a quiet intensity. "None of us did, Jason. But we can't keep playing the blame game. We can't keep pointing fingers at each other. We're all here, still carrying the weight of what happened, and that's not going to change unless we deal with it. Together."

There was a moment of quiet, the weight of Ben's words hanging in the air. The tension didn't dissipate, but the words had struck a chord. They all knew he was right. They couldn't keep doing this, couldn't keep blaming each other for the unraveling of their friendships. They were all complicit in what had happened, and now, they had to face the truth, no matter how painful.

Jason's breath hitched, his face contorted with a mixture of guilt and anger. "I tried," he whispered, more to himself than anyone else. "I tried to keep it together. I didn't want to be the one to fall apart. But I was scared, Ben. I was scared of losing everyone, scared of being the one who didn't have it all figured out. So I pushed everyone away."

Tom's expression softened, but the years of resentment were still there, buried beneath the surface. "You weren't the only one who was scared, Jason. You think we weren't all afraid? You think I didn't want to fix things? But we were all in our own heads, dealing with our own issues, and you didn't let us in. You never let us in."

Jason's eyes flashed with anger, but there was something vulnerable in his gaze too, something that hadn't been there before. "And you think you were any better, Tom? You just shut down. You pretended like everything was fine, like you were fine, but you were just as messed up as the rest of us. We all had our demons, and none of us were willing to face them. I couldn't do it alone. And I don't think any of us could."

The honesty in Jason's words stung, but there was a strange sense of clarity in them too. It was true. They had all been running from the truth, running from each other, afraid to face the mess that had grown between them. They had all been hiding, each one of them trapped in their own struggles, but too proud or too ashamed to ask for help.

Sarah could feel the weight of it pressing down on her. She had always thought that their friendship, their bond, was unbreakable, that no matter what happened, they would always find a way back to each other. But now, looking at them—seeing the pain, the regret, the frustration—she realized that some things couldn't be fixed with just a few conversations. The past had taken its toll, and the scars were too deep to ignore.

As the conversation continued, the group began to unravel further. What had been a painful but necessary confrontation soon turned into a chaotic mess of anger, frustration, and unspoken resentment. Each person, it seemed, was carrying their own version of the story, their own perspective on what had gone wrong. And while some of them were still trying to hold on to the past, to salvage what little was left, others were already pulling away, realizing that the damage might be too great to repair.

"I don't know if I can do this anymore," Emma whispered, her voice breaking. The tears she had been holding back for hours finally fell, her vulnerability raw and painful to witness. "I don't know if I can keep pretending that everything is fine. We're not the same, and we're never going to be the same."

Sarah turned to Emma, her heart aching for her friend. She could see the years of pain in her eyes, the weight of the unresolved issues that had been building for so long. Emma had always been the one to smooth things over, to try to hold the group together, but now she was standing at the precipice, unsure of whether there was anything left to salvage.

"I don't want to be the one to let go," Emma continued, her voice trembling. "But I don't know how to fix this. I don't know if it's even possible."

The words hung in the air, and Sarah knew that they were all facing the same realization. They had tried, so hard, to fix the cracks, to ignore the distance between them, but it was too much. Too much time had passed, too many things had been left unsaid. And now, the walls they had built around themselves were finally crumbling.

It was then that Sarah understood. The clarity she had found earlier in the night wasn't just about herself—it was about the group. She had spent so long trying to recreate something that wasn't there anymore, trying to relive a time when everything felt perfect. But the truth was, they had changed. They had all grown, in different directions, and maybe that was okay.

The most painful truth she had to face was that sometimes, friendships weren't meant to last forever. Sometimes, people grew apart, and that was part of life. The real question wasn't whether they could go back to the way things were—it was whether they were willing to accept that things had changed and that it was time to let go.

"We can't keep pretending," Sarah said, her voice steady, though her heart ached with the weight of her words. "We can't keep trying to fix something that's broken. Maybe it's time to let it go."

The group fell silent, and for the first time that night, there was a sense of understanding. The words were hard to say, but they were necessary. They had all been holding on to something that wasn't there anymore. And maybe, just maybe, it was time to stop pretending and start moving forward.

Chapter VIII: The Turning Point

The air was thick with tension, heavy with words left unsaid and emotions raw from the confrontation. The group had descended into chaos, each person caught in the emotional whirlwind stirred up by Jason and Tom's argument. The damage had been done—anger had been laid bare, regrets spilled out, and no one seemed to know how to pick up the pieces.

But then, a shift occurred. It wasn't loud or dramatic, but it was enough to break the downward spiral. Sarah, sitting in the quiet corner of the group, felt it—a subtle shift in the energy. The storm wasn't over, but it had paused, just long enough for the dust to settle. Everyone was still tense, their minds whirling with the intensity of the confrontation, but for a brief moment, there was a collective understanding that the cycle of blame, anger, and regret needed to stop.

Jason was the first to speak, though his voice was quieter, more subdued than it had been moments earlier. The edge of his anger still lingered, but it was tempered now with something softer—something vulnerable.

"I didn't mean to do this," he said, his voice shaking slightly, the words laced with the exhaustion of having fought too long, too hard. "I didn't want to tear us apart, but that's what I've done. I've pushed everyone away, and I don't even know how to fix it."

Tom, who had been standing off to the side, arms crossed, jaw clenched, finally spoke, his voice measured but tinged with frustration. "You've been holding onto all this anger for so long, Jason. And we've all been afraid to confront it. Afraid to look at the truth. But we can't move forward until we do."

Jason's gaze shifted downward, as if the weight of Tom's words had finally hit him in a way they hadn't before. He looked vulnerable now, no longer the confident, sometimes brash friend who had kept the group together with humor and charisma. He was just a person, broken and regretful, staring into the mess he had helped create.

"I know," Jason murmured. "I know I've messed up, but I don't know how to make it right. I don't know if I can."

There was a quiet pause, and for a moment, it seemed like nothing would happen. Everyone was still processing the emotional weight of the conversation, unsure of how to follow up, unsure of what the next step should be. But then, Emma, who had been silently watching the exchange, stood up and slowly made her way over to Jason. The others watched her, sensing what was about to unfold.

"Jason," she said softly, her voice trembling with something close to empathy, "I know you're hurting, but I need you to hear this." She knelt down in front of him, her face open and sincere. "We've all been running from the truth. And I get it. I get why you did what you did, why you tried to keep everyone at arm's length. But that doesn't make it right. We've all hurt each other, Jason. We've all been carrying things we never talked about. And maybe we should have said something sooner."

Jason's eyes welled up with unshed tears, and he wiped them away roughly, as if ashamed of his vulnerability. "I'm sorry, Emma. I should've been there for you. For all of you. I don't know why I shut down, why I let everything fall apart. But I was afraid. Afraid that if I let anyone in, they'd see who I really was. And that scared the hell out of me."

There was a long silence as Emma processed his words. Her expression softened, and she placed a hand on his arm gently, offering him a quiet comfort that only someone who had known him so well could provide.

"You don't have to apologize for being afraid, Jason," she said, her voice a mixture of sadness and understanding. "But you do have to take responsibility for how your actions hurt us. We all need to do that. I've been angry too, angry that you shut me out, that you didn't trust me enough to let me in."

Jason nodded, looking down at the ground. "I know. And I'm so sorry. I don't know how to fix it. I don't know if we can go back to what we had, but I want to try. I want to rebuild what we lost, even if it's not the same."

Emma gave him a small smile, her eyes filled with a quiet understanding. "Maybe we can't go back to what we were, but maybe we can start something new. Maybe that's the only way forward."

The others were watching now, their expressions softening as the tension began to ebb, replaced by the rawness of apology and regret. Sarah looked around at her friends, her own heart heavy with the weight of everything they had been through, everything that had been left unsaid for so long.

Tom was the next to speak, his voice quieter than it had been before, but still laced with emotion. "I've been angry too, Jason. Angry at you for shutting me out, angry at myself for not saying anything sooner. But the truth is, I was scared too. Scared of what would happen if we faced the truth. Scared of losing everything."

Jason looked up at him, the weight of his regret settling deeper into his chest. "I didn't mean to push you away, Tom. But I didn't know how to be the friend you needed. I didn't know how to be the friend anyone needed."

Tom took a deep breath, exhaling slowly. "I get it, Jason. I do. We've all been running from the same fears, haven't we? The fear of losing each other, the fear of what would happen if we admitted how much we've hurt each other. But we can't keep running. Not anymore."

The group was quiet for a long moment, the weight of what had been said slowly sinking in. There was still so much hurt between them, still so many things left unresolved. But for the first time in a long time, there was the faintest glimmer of hope.

"Maybe we can't fix everything," Jason said, his voice hoarse. "Maybe we can't go back to what we had, but I want to try. I don't want to lose you all. I don't want to lose the people I thought I'd never be without."

There was a shift in the group, a subtle change in the air as each of them, in their own way, began to process what Jason had said. They weren't going to go back to the way things were—they couldn't. But perhaps there was a chance for something new, something they could build from the pieces of the past that still held meaning.

Emma stepped back, giving Jason the space he needed, but her expression remained soft, the anger that had once been so evident now replaced by a quiet sense of understanding. The group, despite everything, had taken the first step toward healing, and it wasn't about undoing the past. It was about facing the truth and acknowledging that, no matter how broken they were, they still had the potential to rebuild.

"I think we've all been running," Sarah said quietly, the weight of her words settling on her like a final realization. "Running from the truth, from the pain, from each other. And maybe that's why we've been stuck for so long. But we can't keep running anymore. We have to face the past, painful as it is, if we want to move forward."

The others nodded, their expressions a mixture of resignation and understanding. No one was expecting an easy fix, no one was pretending that everything could be made right with a few heartfelt apologies. But there was a sense of willingness now—a willingness to try.

For the first time that night, Sarah felt a glimmer of something positive in the air. It wasn't a resolution, not yet, but it was a start. They had begun the hard work of facing the past, and perhaps, just perhaps, they could start to rebuild.

For a brief moment, the group sat in silence, each person lost in their own thoughts. It was a quiet unlike any they had experienced that evening. The air was still, and though there was lingering tension, it felt more like the calm before a storm than the storm itself. The apologies had been made, the regrets expressed, but the weight of the unspoken truth was still hanging over them all. The battle had not yet been won, but something had shifted, and for the first time in a long while, there was a chance for something new to emerge from the wreckage.

Sarah, ever the observer, watched her friends closely. She had always been the one to notice the smallest details, to pick up on the things people didn't say out loud. She could see it now—the subtle shift in their expressions. There was no instant forgiveness. There was no quick resolution. But there was something else: vulnerability. And that was a start. That was a step in the right direction.

She glanced at Emma, who was sitting quietly beside her. Emma's eyes were filled with a mixture of sadness and hope, the two emotions battling for dominance. They had both been through so much together, and though they had shared a moment of healing, Sarah knew that there was still much to face.

"We're not done yet," Sarah said softly, her voice breaking the silence between them. "There's still so much to work through."

Emma nodded, her face thoughtful. "I know. But for the first time, I think we're willing to do the work. That's something."

Sarah looked around at the group—Jason and Tom, who had shared their rawest emotions, still sitting opposite each other, but now quieter, softer. Ben, who had remained mostly silent, was staring into the distance, his expression unreadable. But Sarah could see that he, too, was processing everything. Even if they hadn't spoken the words, they had all felt the shift. They couldn't go back to the way things were, but they could move forward—if they were brave enough to face the truth.

The moment didn't last long. Like most things that required too much emotion, it was fleeting, replaced quickly by the weight of the unresolved. The truth they had faced—while difficult and painful—had begun to settle, and with it came a renewed sense of clarity. But the clarity didn't erase the pain. It didn't erase the betrayal. And it certainly didn't erase the fear.

"I think it's time we talk about what's really going on," Tom said, breaking the silence that had lingered since the apologies. His voice was firm, but there was a weariness to it. He had let go of some of his anger, but not all of it. There was still too much pain, too many scars.

"Tom…" Jason began, but he stopped himself. The words were there, but they felt hollow, like they had already been spoken too many times before. "I'm not sure I can do this again. I don't know if I can keep doing this."

Tom's eyes hardened. "You think I'm asking you to? No. I'm not asking you to do anything. But we can't keep going in circles, pretending like everything is fine when it's not."

Sarah saw it, then—the point of no return. They were nearing it. The threshold where the group would either face the truth of what had happened or splinter, permanently, into pieces too jagged to fit back together. The reality was that the group could not go forward without reckoning with the full scope of what had happened, and it was unclear if they could ever recover from the damage they had done to each other.

"I know," Jason muttered. "I know I've messed up. But the truth is, I don't know if we can fix this. I don't know if we can ever go back to the way things were."

Tom stood up abruptly, a sharp motion that seemed to split the space between them. "You're not listening to me, Jason. It's not about going back. It's about figuring out if we can still move forward. If we can't, if we're all just holding onto a fantasy of what we were, then what the hell is the point of this?"

The intensity of Tom's words seemed to hit everyone at once. The room, still quiet with the aftermath of the confrontation, suddenly felt even more suffocating. It wasn't just the words—they were not just questioning each other's actions, but their very ability to reconcile the past with the future. It wasn't only the emotional wreckage; it was the uncertainty about whether they could find a way to live in a reality that had left them broken and unsure.

There was a long silence after Tom's words, the gravity of the moment sinking in. Sarah realized that the hard truth was beginning to crystallize. The weight of their history was heavy, and while there was a tentative desire to rebuild, there was an equal fear of revisiting all the old pain. There was no easy answer, no simple solution to the rift that had grown between them over the years.

"I think..." Sarah started, her voice hesitant but firm, "I think we need to decide if we're willing to face the cost of trying to fix this."

The others turned to look at her, and she could see the curiosity in their eyes, the longing for clarity. They were all looking for a way forward, but no one knew exactly what that way would look like. Would they be able to accept the truth of what had happened? Would they be able to forgive the betrayals, the hurt, the distance?

"We have to decide if the history we have is worth the pain it might cause to revisit it," Sarah continued. "We've all been running from it for so long. But maybe, to heal, we have to face it fully—no more pretending. No more ignoring what happened."

Emma, still sitting beside Sarah, placed a hand on her shoulder, giving her a small nod of approval. "It's scary," she said softly. "But maybe it's the only way. Maybe we have to see the truth, all of it, to move forward."

Jason's eyes flickered between Sarah and Emma. "And what if it's too much? What if we can't handle it? What if all of this—everything we're trying to fix—isn't worth it?"

"It's worth it if we're willing to try," Sarah replied, her voice steady now. "But we have to be honest. We can't keep pretending. And we can't keep blaming each other for what happened. We have to take responsibility for our own part in this."

The group fell silent again, but this time it wasn't the tense quiet of the moments before the storm—it was a quieter kind of silence. The kind that comes with understanding. They were all grappling with the truth that they might not be able to fully fix what had been broken, but they could start something new. The weight of the past would never be gone, but they didn't have to keep dragging it with them, either.

It wasn't going to be easy. No one was expecting miracles. The apology, the confrontation, the regrets— they didn't fix anything. They only made the reality of their situation clearer. They were all so different now. But they were still here. And maybe, just maybe, they could build something new out of the ashes of what had been.

Sarah looked around at the group, seeing the quiet resolve in their eyes, the uncertainty, and the faint hope. They had come to a turning point. The path ahead wasn't clear, but they had reached an understanding: the past couldn't define them anymore. They had to face the pain, the fear, and the truth of who they were now. And that was the only way forward.

The conversation slowed, the words spoken lingering in the air like the faint echo of a distant storm. The group had reached an unspoken understanding—that they could not keep moving forward without addressing the past. But the silence that followed was heavier than before, and no one spoke for several moments. The weight of their collective history hung around them like a fog, clouding the way ahead. Yet, amid the discomfort, there was something else: a sense of possibility, however fragile it might have been.

Sarah felt a strange sense of clarity in that moment. The path they would take wouldn't be easy, and it certainly wouldn't be without more conflict and pain. But perhaps this was the first step in a long, difficult healing process. They had chosen to face the truth, and with that choice came the responsibility of either breaking apart completely or finding a way to rebuild, piece by fragile piece.

Jason, after a long pause, finally broke the silence, his voice quiet but resolute. "Maybe we can't fix everything, but... maybe we can try. Maybe we can try to be friends again, even if it's not the way we were before."

Tom looked over at him, his expression softening slightly. He had always been the one to hold onto his pride, the one to keep his emotions in check, but tonight, he seemed more open, more willing to let go of the bitterness that had consumed him for so long. "We'll never be the same as we were," he said, his voice measured, "but maybe that's not the point. Maybe it's not about going back to who we were, but about being who we are now, and trying to make that work."

A sense of collective relief washed over the group, though it was tempered by the realization that the real work was only just beginning. They were still far from resolving everything, still far from healing the wounds that had been caused by years of silence, avoidance, and broken promises. But in that moment, they had taken the first step. They had acknowledged the pain, and they had allowed themselves to be vulnerable, to admit that they didn't have all the answers.

Sarah looked around at her friends, each one carrying their own burdens, their own scars. But there was something different now. There was a quiet understanding that perhaps they could rebuild—slowly, carefully, and with great effort—but it was possible. It was a start.

"I don't know if I can forgive everything," Emma said suddenly, her voice barely above a whisper. She had been quiet for much of the conversation, but now, her words carried the weight of unspoken pain. "But maybe forgiveness isn't the point. Maybe we just have to learn how to live with the hurt and still move forward. Together."

There was a collective nod from the group, each person recognizing the truth of Emma's words. Forgiveness wasn't a simple process. It couldn't happen in one conversation, one apology. But understanding, vulnerability, and the willingness to try—those were the first steps toward something new, something that had the potential to heal.

After a long, shared silence, the group began to gather their things, the weight of the conversation still lingering. It wasn't a resolution—there were no guarantees that they would make it through the process of rebuilding, no assurances that their efforts wouldn't crumble under the weight of their unresolved past. But there was a shared sense of determination, something unspoken yet understood by them all.

As Sarah packed her things, she couldn't help but reflect on the years that had passed since they had all been close. So much had changed, so much had been lost, and she wondered if they could ever truly recreate what had once been. The group they had been, the friendship they had shared, was gone. But what they had now—this new version of themselves—could still hold meaning, even if it was painful, even if it wasn't what they had hoped for.

"What happens now?" Jason asked, his voice quieter than it had been earlier, as he stood beside Sarah, looking out at the group. His face was somber, but there was something different in his eyes now—a flicker of hope, perhaps, or at least the willingness to try.

Sarah paused, considering his question. "Now, we keep going. We don't have all the answers, but we don't give up either. We'll take it one step at a time, and maybe we'll find something worth holding onto."

The words felt right, and as Sarah looked around, she saw the others—each one of them carrying their own burdens, their own regrets, but still willing to try. The healing wouldn't be quick. It wouldn't be easy. But they had opened the door to something that had been locked away for far too long.

As the last of the evening's light began to fade, the group gathered one final time by the cabin, standing in a loose circle. No one spoke at first. There was no need for more words. They had said everything they needed to say, and now, all they could do was step forward, uncertain of what the future held but determined to face it together, however fragile their bonds might be.

"I know we've all been through a lot," Sarah said, breaking the silence. Her voice was calm, steady. "And I know it's not going to be easy. But we can't keep pretending. We can't keep running from what happened. But maybe, just maybe, we can move forward. Maybe we can still be in each other's lives, even if it's not the same as before."

Jason nodded, his expression thoughtful. "I don't know what that looks like yet, but I want to try. I don't want to lose this group. I don't want to lose the people who meant so much to me."

Tom's voice was quieter than usual, but there was a new sense of understanding in it. "None of us do. But we can't keep pretending that everything is fine when it's not. We have to accept that things have changed, and that's okay. We just have to decide if we're willing to face the truth together."

Ben, who had been mostly silent up until this point, looked up, his expression a mixture of thoughtfulness and quiet resolve. "I think it's worth it. The past can't define us forever. But the future is ours to shape."

With those words, the group began to disband, slowly and quietly, each person retreating into themselves, processing what had happened, what had been said. There were no grand gestures, no sweeping resolutions. But there was a sense that, despite everything, they had taken a step toward healing.

As Sarah stood there, watching her friends leave, she realized that while the past could never be erased, it could be acknowledged. It could be part of their story, but it didn't have to define their future. The future was still theirs to shape, and it would be shaped by the choices they made, by the willingness to face the truth and move forward together.

And for the first time that evening, Sarah felt a quiet hope stir within her. It wasn't much, but it was something.

Chapter IX: The Breaking Point

It had been days since the emotional breakthrough, since the apologies had been spoken, and while there was a fleeting sense of relief, the cracks that had been exposed couldn't simply be ignored. The group's fragile sense of unity, built on years of friendship and unspoken pain, now felt like a house of cards. Each person was walking a tightrope between the past and the present, unsure of how to balance the two. As time passed, the distance between them seemed to grow instead of shrink.

The final moments of the reunion had arrived, and the group was left to face the aftermath of everything they had tried—and failed—to rebuild. The emotional tension was thick, hanging in the air like a storm that never seemed to pass. No one was willing to admit it, but it was clear that they were reaching the breaking point.

Sarah could feel it in her gut. She had tried to hold on, tried to believe that this reunion would bring them closer, that they could heal together. But as the days wore on, it became harder to deny the truth: some wounds couldn't be repaired. Some relationships were too far gone, too broken to fix with a few honest conversations. And as the final hours of the reunion ticked away, it was becoming painfully clear that they were nearing the end of this chapter—whether they liked it or not.

It started with Emma. Sarah hadn't expected it, not after everything they had shared—the heartfelt apologies, the vulnerable conversations—but when Emma quietly slipped away from the group one afternoon, Sarah couldn't help but notice the way her absence was felt by everyone.

At first, no one said anything. Emma had always been the one to hold things together, to be the glue that bound them all. But now, Sarah realized with a heavy heart, it seemed like Emma had reached her limit. The weight of the past had become too much for her to bear, and the emotional exhaustion of trying to reconcile everything had taken its toll.

"Is Emma... okay?" Sarah asked, her voice barely above a whisper as she caught sight of the others. Her eyes scanned the group, but there was no sign of Emma.

Jason, who had been unusually quiet all day, glanced up from the fire, his eyes tired and distant. "I don't know," he said softly. "She's been distant lately. Like she's... checked out."

Tom, who had been sitting across from them, didn't seem surprised. "She's probably just tired. We all are."

But Sarah knew better. It wasn't just tiredness. It was something deeper. Emma had always been the one to hold everyone together, to act as the mediator when things got tough. But now, the weight of everything they had been through had become too much. And Emma, the one who had always been the rock, had finally cracked under the pressure.

As the hours passed, the group continued to drift apart, the tension mounting. Conversations became sparse, awkward pauses growing longer. The emotional strain was palpable, and the silence between them felt like a chasm too wide to bridge. No one was willing to admit it, but they all knew—the group was breaking.

"I think we need to talk about where we go from here," Ben finally said, his voice steady but heavy with uncertainty. He had been quiet through much of the reunion, observing from the sidelines, but now, the finality in his voice caught everyone's attention.

Sarah turned toward him, surprised by the shift in his tone. Ben had always been the most reserved, the least willing to confront uncomfortable truths. But now, something in his voice carried a weight that couldn't be ignored.

"What do you mean?" Jason asked, looking at Ben, his brow furrowed in confusion. "We've already talked about everything. We've said what we needed to say."

Ben shook his head slowly. "No. I don't think we've really talked about it. Not in the way we need to. We've been pretending that we're all going to magically heal from this, but we're not. Some of us—" He paused, glancing at the others, his voice quieter. "Some of us aren't ready to move on, and some of us don't even want to. And that's okay, but we need to acknowledge it."

The room fell silent again, and for a moment, no one spoke. The truth was out in the open now—the realization that not everyone was on the same page. Some of them were trying to rebuild, to hold on to what had been, while others were already emotionally withdrawing, realizing that some things couldn't be fixed.

It was Jason who spoke next, his voice thick with emotion. "Maybe we can't go back. Maybe we're not the same people anymore, and maybe that's the hardest thing to accept."

His words were a blow to the chest, and Sarah felt the sting of them in her own heart. She had been holding on to the hope that they could salvage something—anything—from their past, but now, she realized, that might not be possible. They had all changed, and not all of them were ready to embrace those changes.

"I can't do this," Jason continued, his voice quieter now, almost pleading. "I can't keep pretending like everything's fine when it's not. I don't know if I even want to fix this."

And with that, the dam broke.

Jason stood up abruptly, his chair scraping against the floor as he made his way toward the door. The rest of the group watched in stunned silence as he walked away, his footsteps echoing in the quiet space.

"Jason, wait!" Sarah called out, but it was too late. The door slammed shut behind him, leaving the group in a state of shock.

The silence that followed Jason's departure was unbearable. No one spoke. No one moved. The weight of the situation had hit them all, and it was too much to ignore. Some of them had been trying to hold on, to believe that this reunion could be the catalyst for healing, but now, it was clear that the cracks were too deep, the wounds too raw.

"I knew this would happen," Tom said, his voice bitter with a mixture of frustration and resignation. "We've been trying to pretend like we can fix everything, but we can't. We can't undo the damage we've done."

Sarah felt a knot tighten in her stomach. It was true. They couldn't undo the past. The damage was done. The group that had once been a source of comfort and security was now divided, with some of them ready to let go and others still clinging to what they had once been. And in that moment, Sarah realized that there was no going back. The reunion, which had once held the promise of healing, had become the point of no return.

As the hours passed, the group sat in silence, each person left alone with their thoughts, their emotions, and the realization that the unity they had once shared was no longer possible. The rift that had grown between them over the years had finally broken open, and now, there was no way to fix it.

"I think it's time to go," Sarah said softly, her voice breaking the silence. She looked around the room, meeting each of their gazes. "We've tried. We've done what we could, but some things are beyond repair. Maybe it's time we accept that."

The others nodded, some reluctantly, others with a sense of finality in their eyes. They had reached the breaking point. There was no more pretending. Some of them would leave this reunion with unresolved pain, and others would walk away knowing that it was time to move on.

As Sarah gathered her things and walked toward the door, she couldn't help but feel a profound sense of loss. This chapter of her life was closing, and though it was painful, it was also necessary. They couldn't keep dragging the past with them. It was time to let go, to move forward, and to accept that not all relationships were meant to last forever.

And as she stepped outside, the cool night air washing over her, she realized that some things—some friendships—are meant to break, so that new beginnings can take shape.

Jason's departure left a hollow silence in the room. It was as though the air had been sucked out of the space, leaving them all suspended in disbelief. No one spoke at first, the weight of the situation settling heavily upon them. They had all known this moment was coming, but now that it was here, it felt like an irreversible fracture, something that couldn't be undone. Jason had walked out, and with him went the last vestiges of the unity they had tried so desperately to hold on to.

Sarah stood frozen by the door, unsure of what to do next. She had always been the one to try to bring people together, to fix things when they seemed broken, but this... this felt beyond her ability to heal. It was as if they had reached the point of no return, a place where even their shared history couldn't hold them together anymore.

"I'm sorry," Tom's voice broke through the silence, soft but heavy with regret. His gaze shifted toward Sarah.

"I didn't mean for it to end like this. I didn't want this to happen."

She turned toward him, her heart aching. "None of us did," she whispered. "But sometimes things just... fall apart."

Ben, who had been standing near the window, finally spoke up, his voice filled with quiet finality. "It's over, isn't it? The way we were. The way we wanted to be."

Sarah nodded slowly, her throat tight with emotion. "Yeah. It is. I think we've been pretending for too long, trying to fix things that can't be fixed."

The group sat in a tense stillness, the room heavy with the weight of their shared truth. They had tried to salvage what was left of their bond, but in doing so, they had overlooked the irreparable damage that had been done over the years. Some of them had been holding on to hope, but now, it was clear that it was time to let go.

After what seemed like an eternity, Emma stood up from her chair, her movements slow and deliberate. She had been quiet for most of the evening, processing everything in silence, but now, there was something in her expression—a quiet resolve—that seemed to shift the energy in the room.

"I can't stay," she said softly, her voice filled with a mixture of sadness and acceptance. "I thought we could fix this, that we could find a way back to what we were. But I can't keep pretending like it's possible. I can't keep hoping for something that isn't there anymore."

Her words felt like a punch to the gut. Sarah had known that Emma was struggling, that she had been torn between the desire to heal and the painful reality that some things couldn't be repaired. But hearing her say it aloud, hearing the finality in her voice, made it all feel so much more real. Emma was done. She had reached her limit, and there was no going back from this.

"I think we all need to accept that," Emma continued, her voice barely above a whisper. "We've changed. All of us. And the friendships we once had... they're not coming back. Not like we want them to."

Tom stood up too, his eyes downcast, his shoulders slumped. "I don't want to leave," he muttered, his voice thick with emotion. "But I'm starting to understand that maybe... maybe we weren't meant to stay the same. Maybe this is just how it has to be."

The words hit Sarah like a wave. They were all coming to terms with something they had tried so hard to avoid: the reality that this reunion, this attempt to rekindle their past, was only prolonging the inevitable. They had been pretending that they could go back to a time when things were easier, when they were all in sync, but that version of themselves no longer existed. Time had changed them, and no amount of nostalgia could bring it back.

The group's unity, which had been fragile at best, was now crumbling completely. Some of them were already pulling away, retreating into themselves, while others were still trying to hold on, trying to salvage whatever was left. The emotional divide was becoming clear, with no middle ground to be found.

"Maybe this was never going to work," Sarah said, her voice shaking with the weight of the words. "Maybe we've been trying to force something that was never meant to be."

Emma walked toward the door, her back to the group, but her words were still sharp, cutting through the heavy silence. "I need to go. I need to find some space.

We've all been holding onto the past for too long, and it's time to let it go."

"I understand," Sarah replied quietly, her heart breaking as she watched Emma make her way to the door. There was no stopping her now. Emma was leaving, and in doing so, she was taking the last thread of hope with her.

Ben, who had been silent until now, finally spoke. "I'm done too," he said softly. "I'm not sure there's anything left here worth holding onto."

The finality of Ben's words struck Sarah deeply. She had never expected him to be the first to walk away, but it was clear now that the emotional withdrawal wasn't just Jason's, wasn't just Emma's. It was happening to all of them. Everyone had reached their breaking point, and now, there was no more pretending. The past was too painful to revisit, and the future seemed too uncertain to navigate together.

As the group began to disperse, Sarah felt the walls close in around her. The hope that she had clung to so desperately was slipping away, and all she could do was watch as the last remnants of their friendship were torn apart.

"We tried," Sarah whispered to herself, her voice barely audible. "We tried to fix what was broken, but maybe it was too broken to fix."

Jason's words echoed in her mind: "WE CAN'T GO BACK. MAYBE WE CAN'T FIX EVERYTHING." Those words had never felt truer than they did now. There was no going back. There was no fixing this. They had all tried, in their own ways, but they had come to the painful realization that sometimes, things couldn't be repaired. Sometimes, people couldn't be fixed.

As Sarah looked around the room, at the empty space left by Emma's absence, at the unspoken tension between Tom and Jason, she realized that this chapter had come to an end. The group, which had once been inseparable, was no longer the same. And while it was painful, while it hurt to let go, she knew it was time.

It was time to move on.

The room was emptier now. The space that had once been filled with laughter, arguments, and the comfort of shared history was now nothing but silence. As the final few members of the group packed their things and said their goodbyes, there was no more anger, no more shouting. Instead, there was an eerie stillness, a resignation that seemed to settle in the air, thick and suffocating. The emotional fallout had begun, and it was far more painful than any confrontation or argument they had ever had.

Sarah stood alone, watching as the last of her friends left, each one silently retreating into the night. They had come together with the hope of rekindling something they once shared. They had tried to fix what was broken, to heal the wounds that had festered for years. But now, as she stood there, the reality was clear: some wounds could never be healed, and some friendships couldn't survive the passage of time.

She felt a tightness in her chest, the weight of the situation pressing down on her, but she didn't cry. She didn't know how to feel anymore. There was no anger, no resentment—just a deep, hollow sadness. This wasn't the reunion she had hoped for, the one where they would all rediscover the closeness they had once shared. Instead, it had become the final chapter, a painful goodbye to something they had all outgrown.

It was late, far later than Sarah had expected, but the night felt endless. She knew the others would be gone by now—Emma, Ben, Jason, Tom—each of them had made their own decisions about what was best for them, and that was the hardest part. They weren't abandoning her. They weren't rejecting her. They were rejecting the idea of going back to a time that could never exist again. They were rejecting the fantasy of restoring what had been.

As she sat down on the porch steps, the chill of the night creeping in, Sarah closed her eyes for a moment, letting the quiet settle over her. There was no sound but the rustling of leaves in the trees and the soft chirping of insects in the distance. It felt like the world was moving on without her, leaving her behind in the stillness. And maybe, she thought, that was how it was always meant to be.

The group was no more. The friendships they had shared, the history they had built, were all fragments of a past that no longer fit who they had become. It wasn't about them being bad people or choosing the wrong paths. It was about the reality that sometimes people outgrow each other, and no matter how much they tried, they couldn't go back to who they once were.

Sarah stood up, the weight of the night pressing down on her, and started walking back into the house. The silence was overwhelming, but she knew there was nothing left to say. They had all tried, and now, it was time to accept the truth.

The next morning, Sarah woke to the faint light of dawn breaking through the window. The house was still, as if frozen in time, reflecting the emotional stillness that had settled over her since the night before. The others were gone. There was no final confrontation, no closure. Just silence. She had spent so many years clinging to the idea of the past, to the friendships that had once meant everything to her, but now she knew: it was time to let go.

She went to the kitchen, making herself a cup of coffee as the sun slowly began to rise. The house felt cold, empty, as though it had lost its warmth the moment the last of her friends had left. The memories they had shared—the laughter, the inside jokes, the late-night talks—had been overshadowed by the pain of their unraveling.

But even in the silence, even in the emptiness, there was a sense of clarity. She wasn't sure where the future would lead her, but for the first time in a long time, she knew she couldn't keep living in the past. She couldn't keep holding onto relationships that no longer existed, and she couldn't keep trying to fix something that was too broken to be repaired.

Sarah sat at the kitchen table, her hands wrapped around the warm mug of coffee, the steam rising in delicate swirls. She wasn't sure what the next step was, but she knew she had to keep moving forward. The past was gone, and no amount of wishing or hoping would bring it back.

As she gazed out the window, watching the light of the day grow brighter, she made a silent promise to herself: she would stop looking back. She would let go of the people who no longer fit into her life and embrace the future, even though it was uncertain and unfamiliar. It wouldn't be easy. Letting go never was. But for the first time, she felt a glimmer of hope.

She had spent so much time trying to restore what had been lost, but now, she realized that the future couldn't be shaped by the past. She would have to build something new, something that was her own. And that scared her, but it also excited her in a way she hadn't felt in years.

She stood up from the table, placing the mug down with quiet finality. The group she had once known, the friends she had once relied on, were gone, but in their absence, there was space for something new. Something that would be hers to shape.

With one last glance at the house, Sarah took a deep breath and stepped out into the morning sunlight. She didn't know what the future held, but for the first time, she felt ready to face it.

Chapter X: Introspection

The sun had barely risen when Sarah decided to take a walk. The weight of the previous days, of the painful confrontations and the final, unavoidable separation, had settled heavily in her chest. She had spent the night in a quiet daze, reflecting on everything that had happened, but today, she needed space. The quiet of the early morning seemed like the only place where she could think clearly, without the overwhelming hum of unresolved emotions or the guilt of feeling like she should have done more.

The air was cool, crisp against her skin, and as she walked down the path that led from the house, the stillness around her felt almost comforting. The leaves rustled in the trees, their movements gentle in the early morning breeze. She breathed deeply, trying to fill her lungs with the freshness of the air, as if in doing so, she could somehow clear her mind.

She had spent so many years trying to hold on to what she had with her friends, trying to recreate the bond they once shared, but now, walking down that familiar path, she realized something painful: the people they had been, the group they once were, was gone. The friends she had known in her youth—those friends who had been with her through every significant moment—were no longer the people who stood before her in the reunion. Time had changed them, and it had changed her, too.

Her footsteps faltered, and for a moment, she paused, looking out over the landscape. The world felt different, as though she was seeing it with new eyes. The past had been a tether, holding her in place, keeping her from moving forward. But now, she understood. The future was hers to shape. And it was time to let go of the past, of the people who no longer fit into her life.

As Sarah continued her walk, she thought back to the days before the reunion, to the life she had built in the years since they had all drifted apart. She had convinced herself that the reunion would be a chance to rekindle something that had been lost, to re-establish the connections that had once meant everything to her. But the reality had been different. The tension, the anger, the unresolved pain—all of it had come flooding back. It was clear now that trying to recreate the past was a futile endeavor. People change. And so do relationships.

The memories she had cherished—the late-night talks, the shared secrets, the laughter—they were still there, but they no longer had the power to define her. She had been so caught up in trying to fix what had been broken, trying to patch together the rifts in her friendships, that she had failed to recognize the most important truth: the people they had been were not the people they were now. And that was okay.

Sarah smiled sadly to herself, her footsteps slowing as she approached a quiet bench near the edge of a small clearing. She sat down, folding her arms around her knees, as the weight of the past settled heavily in her chest. She wasn't angry. She wasn't resentful. But she was grieving. Not just for the loss of the friendships, but for the person she had been, the person she thought she was supposed to be.

As she sat there, her mind drifted to memories of the past, images flashing before her eyes like old photographs. The first time she met Jason, his easy charm drawing her in like a magnet. The summer nights spent talking with Emma, the long walks in the park where they shared their hopes and dreams, each of them promising to stay connected no matter what. Ben's quiet presence, always steady, always there when needed. Tom's sarcastic humor, his sharp wit that could always make her laugh, even when things were tough.

They had been inseparable, a tight-knit group, bound by the shared experiences of youth. They had supported each other through the highs and lows of growing up, and for a time, it had felt like they would always be there for each other.

But time changes everything. The things they once shared had started to fray around the edges, worn down by distance, by unspoken resentments, by the changing paths of their lives. It wasn't one moment that caused the rift. It wasn't one betrayal or one falling out. It was the slow, inevitable pull of time that had shifted them all, changed them all in ways they couldn't have predicted.

For Sarah, it had been a gradual process. She had gone off to college, found her own place in the world, made new friends. Slowly, the distance between her and the group grew. The letters and phone calls became fewer, the visits less frequent. There were times when she had wondered if she was the one who had drifted away, if she had stopped fighting to keep the connections strong. But the truth was, they had all changed. And with that change, came the recognition that they had all outgrown the relationships they had once shared.

Sarah closed her eyes, resting her head on her knees, as the wind gently tousled her hair. She had spent so much of her life trying to hold onto the past, trying to keep things the way they were. But she had to accept now that some things couldn't be held onto. People couldn't be held onto. She couldn't force her friends to be who they once were. She couldn't force herself to be that person, either.

The reunion had forced her to confront the truth of that, to see it clearly for the first time. She wasn't the same person she had been when they were all close. And neither were they. The connections that had once been so strong, so unshakable, had been altered by time, by distance, by the choices they had made. It wasn't anyone's fault. It wasn't about blame. It was simply the way things were.

The hardest part was accepting that. Accepting that she couldn't keep living in the shadow of who she had once been, or who they had once been together. There was no going back. But there was still forward. There was still a future to be shaped, a life to be built.

For the first time in days, Sarah felt a sense of peace wash over her. The tightness in her chest loosened, the knot of grief and regret slowly uncoiling. She couldn't change the past, but she could change the future. She didn't need the validation of those friendships to define her. She didn't need to fix what was broken. She could build something new—something uniquely hers.

The path ahead wasn't clear, and she didn't know exactly what it would look like. But she knew she had the power to shape it. She had spent so much time looking back, trying to force a return to what was, that she had neglected the opportunity to create something new, to move forward in a way that was true to who she was becoming.

She stood up from the bench, feeling the cool wind brush against her face, the promise of a new beginning in the air. The past was still a part of her—those memories, those friendships, the people she had once shared her life with. But now, she realized, it didn't have to define her. She was ready to move forward, to embrace whatever came next, without the burden of trying to hold onto what was no longer meant to be.

As she walked back toward the house, the world seemed different. The path she had been walking was no longer clouded by regret, by the need to hold onto something that was already gone. She was ready to walk into the future, with the lessons of the past in her heart but not as her anchor.

She didn't need to fix everything. She didn't need to keep holding on. All she needed to do now was embrace the person she had become—and the person she was still becoming.

As Sarah walked back toward the house, the path felt less burdened than before. The weight that had pressed down on her chest for so long had eased, even if only just a little. There were still moments where the past would creep back in, still times when the memories would be sharp, and the loss would sting. But for now, in this moment, Sarah felt something she hadn't in a long time: a quiet, gentle acceptance.

The past could never be undone, but she had the power to choose what to do with the lessons it had taught her. She had spent too many years clinging to the hope of rekindling something that had changed, something that no longer served her. And now, as she stood at the precipice of a new beginning, Sarah realized that perhaps the greatest gift she could give herself was to stop trying to reclaim the past and start living for the present.

Her mind wandered back to the reunion, to the painful moments of confrontation and raw honesty. It had been a brutal but necessary reckoning. And while the group's attempt to reconcile had been short-lived, it had not been without value. It had forced Sarah—and everyone else—to confront who they had become, and that was the first step toward moving on.

There was no denying that letting go of the people they once were had been difficult. The friendships that had once seemed unbreakable were now reduced to fractured memories, and the grief of that loss had been harder to carry than she had expected. But Sarah knew, deep down, that it was time to accept the truth: not all relationships were meant to last forever. And that didn't make them any less important.

As she entered the house, Sarah went to the window and looked out across the landscape. The sun had risen fully now, the golden light spilling across the earth, illuminating everything in its path. The view was breathtaking, yet she couldn't help but think how many times she had missed moments like this, too wrapped up in what had been.

She thought back to her younger self—the girl who had felt invincible, the one who believed that the bonds of friendship could withstand anything. She had been so sure of herself, so certain that nothing could change the tight-knit circle they had formed. But time, as it always does, had changed things.

Sarah had changed, too. She wasn't the same person she had been in those carefree days. She had faced challenges, had grown, had experienced heartache and joy. The person she was now wasn't better or worse than the person she had been then; she was simply different. And maybe that was the point. Life was about growth. It was about change. It was about learning to accept what you can't control and finding peace in the process.

The house behind her—once filled with laughter and the clamor of shared memories—was now empty. The quiet that enveloped the space felt foreign, and yet, it felt right. The reunion had been an attempt to cling to something that wasn't there anymore. But Sarah realized that what was left wasn't brokenness. It was an opportunity for new growth. Her life, just like the house, had room for new things, new people, and new experiences.

Sarah sat down at the kitchen table, letting the warmth of the sunlight seep into her skin. She closed her eyes for a moment, letting the peacefulness of the morning wash over her. There was no rush now. No need to go anywhere, to fix anything. The world was simply unfolding, and for once, Sarah didn't feel the need to control it.

Her mind drifted back to her friends—the ones who had left, the ones who had stayed, and those who had chosen to walk away. They had been such a huge part of her life, and letting go of them, in this sense, felt like a small death. But it was also the birth of something new—a new chapter in her life that she could shape for herself.

She had spent so many years trying to fit into a mold that no longer fit her. She had tried to stay connected to people whose lives had moved on, whose paths had diverged from hers. And while she still loved them—always would, no matter what—she knew that it was time to embrace the person she was becoming. And that person, she realized, wasn't defined by anyone else. She had to choose to be who she was, in this moment, and that meant letting go of the version of herself that had been tethered to the past.

The silence around her was no longer oppressive. It was a space for renewal, a space for Sarah to explore who she was beyond the friendship group she had once known, beyond the expectations of who others thought she should be. She was a person unto herself, and she had the power to define her future.

As the hours passed, Sarah felt the past loosen its grip on her, not in one sudden burst of relief, but in a quiet realization that she could hold on to the good memories without needing to recreate them. The past would always be a part of her—those friends, those experiences, the love and laughter they had shared—would remain in her heart as part of the fabric of who she was. But they no longer needed to be her anchor. She didn't need them to keep moving forward.

She didn't need to fix what was broken. She didn't need to revisit the past in the hope of recapturing something that was lost. The friendships that had slipped away had left her with valuable lessons: about forgiveness, about vulnerability, about the passage of time, and about the strength it takes to let go. And while the ache of loss would always be there, she had learned that it was not the end of the story. It was merely a chapter, one that had run its course.

Sarah looked at her reflection in the kitchen window. She wasn't perfect. She wasn't whole. But she was becoming.

The decision to let go was never easy. It wasn't about forgetting or erasing the past. It was about embracing the change, acknowledging the losses, and moving forward with an open heart, ready to face whatever came next. She knew that there would be more heartache, more loss, more moments of doubt. But she also knew that she was capable of handling it. She had been through worse, and she had come out stronger on the other side.

The future was unknown, and that was both terrifying and exciting. The person she had been with her old friends wasn't the person she was now. But the person she was becoming was someone she could finally be proud of.

And with that acceptance, Sarah stepped away from the window, her heart lighter than it had been in a long time. She didn't know where the road ahead would lead, but for the first time, she was ready to walk it, knowing that she would never have to walk it alone again. The future was hers to shape.

As Sarah spent more time reflecting on everything that had transpired, a sense of calm settled within her. She had been in such a rush to fix everything—to mend relationships that had already frayed beyond repair—that she had forgotten to look inward. But now, as she sat alone in the quiet house, she realized that fixing wasn't always the solution. Sometimes, the only way forward was to accept the reality of what had changed and find peace in the present.

The quiet felt different now. It was no longer the oppressive silence of regret or loss. It was a space filled with possibilities, with the potential for new beginnings. The house, once filled with the noise of her friends' laughter and conversations, now felt like a blank canvas, ready to be filled with her own story.

Sarah stood up and walked to the window again, gazing out at the landscape. The morning sun was high in the sky, casting its golden light across the earth, bathing everything in warmth. She realized that she had been living in the shadows of the past for far too long. It was time to step into the light of her own future, to stop looking back and start looking forward.

It wasn't just about the group of friends she had once had. It was about her entire life, about the expectations she had carried for so long. The idea of who she thought she should be, the person everyone expected her to be, was something she had outgrown. And yet, for so long, she had clung to that version of herself, afraid of what would happen if she let go.

But now, she understood. She had the freedom to be whoever she wanted to be. She didn't have to answer to anyone but herself. And that freedom, while terrifying at first, was also exhilarating. It was the freedom to choose her own path, to write her own story, without the weight of old expectations or broken relationships holding her back.

She knew it wouldn't be easy. There would still be moments when the past would tug at her heart, when the ache of loss would resurface. But she also knew that the pain wasn't something to fear. It was something to embrace, because it was part of the process of healing. It was part of becoming who she was meant to be.

As Sarah stepped outside, she felt the warmth of the sun on her skin, the coolness of the breeze against her face. The world was alive around her, and for the first time in a long time, she felt fully present in it. She wasn't holding on to the past, wasn't waiting for something that would never return. She was here. And that was enough.

Her journey wasn't over, and it would never be a straight path. There would be bumps along the way, moments of doubt, moments of grief. But there would also be moments of joy, of discovery, of growth. And it was all hers to experience.

She walked down the path toward the garden, her steps light, her heart open. She didn't know what the future held, but she knew she was ready for it. She had spent so many years looking back, but now, she was ready to look forward.

There were still things she needed to process, still parts of herself that needed healing. But she was no longer afraid of that. The journey ahead was hers to take, and she was ready to embrace it with open arms.

That afternoon, Sarah decided to make a choice. She chose to move forward, to let go of the past, and to fully embrace the life that was unfolding in front of her. She wasn't running from her memories—she was simply allowing them to be what they were: part of her story, but not the whole story.

She picked up the phone and called a friend she hadn't spoken to in a while. It was a simple gesture, but it felt significant. It was a reminder that she still had the power to make connections, to build new relationships, to create a future that was her own. She had spent so long holding on to what had been, but now she was ready to embrace what could be.

The conversation was easy, comfortable, and filled with laughter. It was a stark contrast to the tension she had felt during the reunion, but it was the kind of connection she had missed. And for the first time in a long time, she realized that the relationships she was meant to have were the ones she had yet to create, the ones that would grow naturally and authentically, without the baggage of the past.

That evening, as Sarah sat alone in the quiet house, watching the stars begin to twinkle in the night sky, she felt a profound sense of peace. She had let go of the past, not with resentment, but with a sense of acceptance. The friendships she had once cherished were no longer part of her life, and that was okay. She had learned from them. They had shaped her, and they would always be a part of her story. But now, it was time to move forward.

She smiled softly to herself, knowing that the journey ahead would not be easy, but it would be hers to navigate. She had the power to choose how she moved forward, and for the first time in a long time, that felt empowering. The future was uncertain, yes, but it was also full of possibility. And Sarah was ready to embrace whatever came next.

Chapter XI: Full Circle

The sun was beginning to set, casting a warm orange glow over the landscape. Sarah stood at the same bench in the garden where she had sat so many days ago, before the reunion had even started. Back then, she had been filled with uncertainty, clinging to memories of a past that no longer fit the person she had become. She had walked down that path, hoping for something to change, something to return. But now, standing here, the feeling was different.

The garden stretched out before her, the flowers blooming in quiet beauty, the trees standing tall as if they had witnessed the passage of time without ever truly changing. There was something calming about the stillness, something that echoed the way Sarah felt inside now. In the beginning, she had been searching for something that had already slipped away, but now, she understood that it wasn't about going back—it was about moving forward, in peace.

She reached down and touched one of the flowers, feeling the softness of the petals under her fingers. It was a symbol, she realized—of both the past and the future. The flowers in the garden had been here long before she arrived, just as the memories of her past would always be a part of her. But they were growing, evolving, just as she was. The garden had a sense of balance, a rhythm that felt both eternal and ever-changing. And Sarah, too, had found a balance between who she had been and who she was becoming.

As she looked around, Sarah's eyes landed on a spot in the garden she hadn't noticed before. A small wooden bench, weathered with age, tucked away beneath the branches of an old oak tree. It looked almost identical to the bench where she had sat days ago, the one where she had first begun her reflections. The sense of symmetry struck her deeply. It was a quiet reminder that some things in life don't change, and that's okay.

The bench, much like the group she had once known, had weathered time. It had endured the shifting seasons, the changes in the landscape, and yet it still had a purpose. It still offered a place for rest, for reflection, for quiet moments of peace. And in the same way, Sarah had learned to accept that some parts of her past were still with her, shaping who she was but not defining her future.

She took a step toward the bench and sat down, feeling the coolness of the wood beneath her. The familiar scent of earth and flowers filled her senses, grounding her in the present. This was the place where she had spent so much time wishing for things to be different, for things to return to how they once were. But now, sitting there, she felt a sense of completion.

Everything had changed. The friendships, the relationships, even her own identity had evolved. But that was the natural course of life. Nothing stayed the same, and trying to hold onto the past could only cause pain. She had learned that lesson. And now, in this moment, Sarah felt a deep sense of peace. She was no longer defined by the past. She was defined by who she was now—and who she was still becoming.

As the evening sky deepened into dusk, Sarah's thoughts drifted to the reunion, to the people she had once been so close to, to the pain and the growth that had come with their separation. She thought of Emma, Tom, Ben, and Jason—each of them, in their own way, had been part of her journey. Their shared history would always be with her, but she no longer felt the need to try to fix what had been broken. She had accepted the past and the people they had all become, and she had let go.

It was only now, sitting in the stillness of the garden, that she realized how much she had changed. The person who had walked into that reunion, desperate to restore something that had slipped through her fingers, was not the person sitting here now. She had learned to let go, to embrace change, and to accept that closure didn't always come with a grand gesture or a dramatic reconciliation. Sometimes, it came with a quiet moment of peace, a moment where you realized that the past had shaped you, but it no longer controlled you.

Sarah looked out at the horizon, where the last slivers of sunlight were fading into the night. She didn't need to know exactly what the future held. She didn't need to have all the answers. But she knew one thing: she was ready for it.

For the first time in a long time, Sarah felt like she had come full circle. The journey that had begun with uncertainty, confusion, and a deep yearning for something that had been lost had led her here—to a place of peace, of acceptance, and of readiness for what came next. The past no longer loomed over her like a shadow. It was part of her story, but it wasn't her story. The story she was writing now was hers to shape, and that filled her with a quiet confidence.

As the stars began to twinkle in the darkening sky, Sarah closed her eyes for a moment, feeling the cool breeze against her face. She had spent so long holding on to something that was gone, but now, she was ready to move forward. Ready to embrace the future, ready to build something new from the lessons of the past.

This was the beginning of her next chapter, and for the first time in a long time, Sarah felt the weight of the past fall away. She had let go, and in doing so, she had made space for something new to grow.

As Sarah sat in the garden, the last remnants of daylight gently fading into twilight, she felt a quiet stillness settle deep within her. The world around her had grown calm, and she could hear nothing but the rustling of leaves and the distant hum of the evening. It was as if the universe had paused for a moment, allowing her to fully absorb the weight of what had transpired, the journey she had been on, and the person she had become.

This was the space where healing had taken place, the space between the past and the future, where time slowed just long enough for Sarah to feel the full impact of her journey. She thought back to everything she had experienced: the heartache, the growth, the moments of doubt, and the moments of clarity. She had learned, in ways she hadn't anticipated, that healing didn't always come quickly. Sometimes, it came slowly, over time, in quiet, subtle moments like this one.

The group she had once known, the friends who had been her family for so long, were no longer a part of her present life. But that didn't mean they were gone forever. They had shaped her, had helped mold her into the person she was today. And she would always carry them with her, not as a source of longing, but as a part of her own growth. She had been shaped by the past, yes, but it was not the past that would define her future.

Her gaze lingered on the garden, the flowers now dimly lit by the soft glow of the evening. It reminded her that just as the seasons change, so did she. There was beauty in every phase, every transition. Nothing stayed the same, and that was a truth she had learned to embrace. The future, though uncertain, was full of potential, full of the possibility of new relationships, new beginnings, and new paths to follow.

The sound of birds returning to their nests for the night filled the air as Sarah stood up from the bench, stretching her legs and feeling the stillness of the evening settle in her bones. She had been here before, in this place of quiet reflection, but she was different now. The journey she had taken had led her here—not to a place of finality, but to a place of readiness. Ready for whatever would come next.

She walked back to the house, feeling the weight of her decision to let go. The past had shaped her, but it didn't own her. She wasn't tied to old versions of herself or to people who no longer fit into her life. She had grown. She had learned. And now, she was ready to move forward, not with anger or regret, but with acceptance.

There was a calmness in her steps as she entered the house, as if each movement she made was part of a new rhythm, one that no longer clung to the shadows of the past. The house felt different, too. It was still the same house she had spent so many memories in, but now it felt like a space for new beginnings, for fresh starts, for the future she was about to embrace.

As Sarah closed the door behind her, she smiled softly to herself. She had reached the point of no return, but it wasn't a sad ending. It was a new beginning—a new chapter in her life that she was ready to step into.

That evening, Sarah sat down by the window, looking out at the stars above. The world outside was peaceful, and so was she. She didn't need to know exactly what the future held. What she had learned over the past days and weeks was that the future would come, whether she was ready or not. But she had everything she needed within her to face it.

The lessons of the past had taught her that sometimes the hardest thing to do is to let go. But letting go had brought her peace, had given her space to grow and to become the person she was meant to be. The friendships of her youth had been beautiful, but they were no longer part of the story she was writing. And that was okay. They had served their purpose, and she had learned from them. Now, it was her turn to step forward, to find her own way, her own path.

She closed her eyes for a moment, feeling the quiet presence of the evening around her. There was no more fear. No more longing. There was just a deep sense of peace, a quiet acceptance of who she had been and who she was becoming.

As the night grew deeper, Sarah stood up and moved toward the door. The future was ahead of her, full of uncertainty, but also full of possibility. She wasn't waiting for anything. She wasn't searching for someone or something to fill the empty space. The emptiness wasn't something to fear. It was the space where new things could grow.

Sarah stepped outside again, her feet firm against the earth beneath her, and she took a deep breath. She felt light. She felt ready. Ready to step into a future that was her own, a future shaped by the lessons she had learned, by the person she had become.

The stars above were endless, a vast expanse of possibility. And Sarah, for the first time in a long time, felt like she could truly embrace it. She had come full circle, from the uncertainty of the past to the peace of the present, and now she was stepping into the future, unafraid and whole.

Summary

In this character-driven drama, we follow Sarah, a woman who has spent much of her life holding on to the friendships and memories of her past. The story centers around her reunion with a group of childhood friends—Jason, Emma, Tom, and Ben—who have all drifted apart over the years due to time, distance, and unresolved tensions. The narrative explores Sarah's internal and external journey as she grapples with the shifting dynamics of her relationships and her own personal growth. The story is not just about a group of friends coming together; it is about Sarah's path to self-acceptance, healing, and ultimately, moving forward.

The story begins with Sarah, who is struggling to reconcile the friendships of her past with the people her friends have become. She believes that reconnecting with them might bring back the sense of unity and purpose she once felt. Sarah is nostalgic for the bonds she once shared with Jason, Emma, Tom, and Ben—their carefree youth, the late-night talks, and the promises they made to always stay connected no matter what life threw at them. However, as the reunion unfolds, Sarah quickly realizes that the people they were back then no longer exist.

In an attempt to rekindle the magic of their youth, Sarah arranges a reunion at a cabin. The gathering is marked by initial awkwardness, but slowly, the group begins to reminisce about their past and share old memories. These moments are filled with warmth, but there is an undercurrent of tension as each person grapples with the fact that they have changed. The group is no longer a tight-knit unit, and some of the bonds that once held them together are now strained by resentment, guilt, and the passage of time.

As the weekend progresses, the group's unity starts to crumble. The story's turning point occurs when Jason and Tom, once the closest of friends, have a heated confrontation. The confrontation brings to the surface old grudges, misunderstandings, and betrayals that have been buried for years. Jason accuses Tom of abandoning him during a difficult time in his life, while Tom fires back, accusing Jason of being selfish and self-absorbed. The exchange grows increasingly intense, and the group is forced to confront the uncomfortable truth that the friendships they had once shared are no longer as unbreakable as they once believed.

Sarah watches as the cracks in the group's dynamics deepen. She is torn between wanting to fix the fractures and realizing that some wounds may be too deep to heal. The group, which once had a clear sense of belonging and identity, is now divided emotionally. The emotional fallout from this confrontation leads to a period of withdrawal for some characters, and Sarah begins to understand that no amount of nostalgia can undo the changes that have taken place over the years.

While some of the group members, like Jason, are still desperate to salvage their relationships, others, like Emma and Ben, begin to pull away. They realize that it might be better to let go of what no longer fits. In these moments of painful clarity, Sarah starts to see that perhaps she, too, needs to let go of the idea of going back to what was. It is during this period of emotional withdrawal that Sarah has her first true moments of introspection, realizing that moving forward might require her to leave behind the people who no longer align with who she has become.

As the group breaks apart, Sarah begins to reflect on her own journey. She grapples with the realization that the friendships she has been trying to hold onto no longer define her. She is no longer the person she was when she first met Jason, Emma, Tom, and Ben. The person she has become, shaped by her experiences, her personal growth, and the relationships she has built over the years, is vastly different. She starts to accept that it's not just her friends who have changed, but that she, too, has transformed. This is a key moment in the story—Sarah's realization that her identity is not tethered to her past, nor is it bound by the people who once played such an important role in her life.

Through quiet moments of reflection, Sarah revisits memories of her childhood and the early days of her friendships with the group. These flashbacks are bittersweet—they serve as reminders of what once was, but also highlight how much has been lost over the years. They also bring Sarah a sense of peace, as she begins to understand that letting go of these relationships doesn't mean erasing the past. Rather, it means accepting it for what it was, appreciating the role it played in shaping her, and finding a way to move forward.

Sarah's introspection also leads her to recognize the limitations of trying to fix things that are beyond repair. There is a sense of relief in this realization. She has spent so much of her life trying to recapture something she could never fully reclaim. But now, she understands that her future lies in embracing the present and the possibilities it offers. This realization marks a pivotal moment in Sarah's emotional journey—she no longer needs the approval or validation of her past relationships to feel whole.

The reunion finally ends in quiet finality. The friends who once shared everything have now gone their separate ways, emotionally and physically. Some leave with a sense of closure, others with unresolved pain. For Sarah, it is a time of bittersweet reflection. She knows that the group she once cherished is gone, but she also understands that it's time to let go. This realization is not easy, but it is necessary. It is the final act of self-acceptance. Sarah has to accept the past for what it is and stop chasing the ghosts of who they once were.

As Sarah begins to step away from the shadow of the past, she takes a step toward the future. This chapter in her life is closing, but there is still much to be written. The emotional fallout from the reunion, the confrontations, and the final moments of withdrawal have brought Sarah to a place of quiet peace. She is no longer fighting the changes in her life; she is accepting them. And this acceptance is freeing.

The ending of the story brings Sarah full circle, symbolizing not just the end of a chapter, but the beginning of something new. Sarah's journey has been one of personal growth, of learning to let go, of discovering who she truly is without the weight of the past holding her back. The story ends on a hopeful note, with Sarah standing at the threshold of her future, ready to embrace it with the lessons of her past in her heart, but no longer controlled by them.

This character-driven drama is rich with themes of self-acceptance, growth, and the bittersweet nature of closure. Sarah's emotional journey is one of learning to navigate the complexities of her relationships and, ultimately, her own identity. The tension between the past and the present drives the narrative, highlighting how our memories and relationships shape us, but how we must also learn to let go of what no longer serves us in order to move forward.

The reunion serves as a catalyst for self-discovery, forcing Sarah and the other characters to confront their own personal truths. Each character's journey is unique, and their choices reflect the emotional complexities of dealing with loss, regret, and the passage of time. Ultimately, the story is about finding peace within oneself and accepting the changes that come with life's natural progression. Sarah's ability to accept the past, forgive herself and others, and embrace the unknown future provides a sense of closure and growth, both for herself and the story as a whole.

In the end, the book is about the quiet, powerful realization that we are not defined by our past or by the relationships we have had, but by how we choose to move forward. The growth that Sarah undergoes is not just emotional—it is a spiritual one. She has learned to forgive, to let go, and to be at peace with the person she has become, even if that means leaving behind the people she once thought would always be in her life. And in this quiet act of self-acceptance, Sarah finds the freedom to live her own story.

ABOU T THE AUTHOR

Roshawn Nixon, a 45-year-old author of Asian descent, is known for his introspective and relatable writing, often exploring themes of identity, personal growth, and relationships. Growing up in a clash of tradition and modernity, Roshawn developed a deep understanding of the struggles faced by individuals trying to reconcile cultural heritage with contemporary society. This influence is evident in his literary voice. Roshawn's love of literature began early in life, finding comfort in the written word. Raised in an Asian household focused on education and discipline, he developed a natural curiosity about the world. As a teenager, he was drawn to stories delving into human emotions and conflicts, which later shaped his writing style. In his twenties, Roshawn expanded his academic horizons by studying literature, psychology, and philosophy. These studies, along with his exposure to both Eastern and Western authors, deepened his perspective, and his writing became more introspective. He aims to inspire readers with stories that reflect human nature, social dynamics, and personal struggles. His debut novel, *Full Circle*, explores themes of friendship, identity, and growing up. The story, about childhood friends reuniting after years of separation, is a poignant journey of self-reflection, emotional understanding, and the bittersweetness of letting go. Known for creating compelling, multidimensional characters, Roshawn's writing highlights personal growth, emotional healing, and the search for meaning in a changing world. His prose is both lyrical and authentic, blending cultural influences seamlessly. In addition to novels, Roshawn writes essays and short stories, addressing topics like culture and personal identity. His emotionally rich work has garnered critical acclaim and continues to resonate with readers. Roshawn's storytelling inspires others to embrace their complexities and find peace in growth and self-acceptance. for 12 seconds.

Roshawn Nixon is a 45-year-old author whose work delves into themes of identity, personal growth, and the complexities of relationships. Raised in a culturally diverse environment where tradition met modernity, he discovered his passion for storytelling at an early age. His academic journey in literature, psychology, and philosophy, enriched by both Eastern and Western influences, has shaped his introspective writing style. His debut novel, "Full Circle," captures the bittersweet process of reconnecting with old friends while confronting inevitable change. Through vivid characters and reflective prose, Roshawn Nixon invites readers to explore the transformative power of self-acceptance and the courage to move forward.

Made in United States
Troutdale, OR
05/10/2025